WESTERN

CHAPTER 1

Gabriel Miller watched the stranger approach, with no particular misgivings. At a distance, there was nothing about him to justify concern. Middle Texas had its share of drifters, mostly out-of-work cowboys, men looking for opportunity in a cattle economy suffering from years of drought and beef-glutted Eastern markets. A decade after the war, tens of thousands of ex-Confederates who had been displaced by poorly managed Reconstruction policies and carpetbagger greed still roamed the South, seeking ways to make a living. Therefore a lone cowboy riding toward Eagle Springs on this wintry December day was hardly cause for alarm. Gabe merely gave the rider a passing glance as he closed the door to the tiny sheriff's office, his mind occupied with other things. The sheriff job was part-time — mostly serving official papers from the county seat over at Gatesville — and paid a meager fifteen dollars a month for what amounted to a few hours of work a week.

Gabe had locked the door and pocketed the key before he gave the stranger a second look. Though he was only nineteen, Gabe considered himself a good judge of men. Back in the spring, when the county judge was preparing to conduct the swearing-in ceremony giving Gabe his legal authority, he had expressed some concerns over his age. Gabe had reminded Judge Green that Eagle Springs really wasn't much of a town . . . there was seldom, if ever, any real trouble there. He had been elected to the job, proof that the townspeople believed he was old enough to handle the duties.

He examined the horseman's face as the newcomer rode up Main Street. Gabe could see in the shadow below the brim of a sweat-stained Confederate cavalry hat a handlebar mustache, a square jaw, and a cold stare that sent a slight chill down his spine. He shoved his hands into the pockets of his old woolen greatcoat to wait for the rider to come abreast of the office. Only then did he notice the bulge of a gun inside the long canvas duster the stranger wore. Though Gabe didn't consider himself a superstitious man, he sensed trouble.

The blue roan gelding bearing the hard-faced traveler halted in front of the office steps, requiring only a slight pull on the reins. The stranger nodded once, a spare greeting, while his pale blue eyes appraised Gabe.

"You the sheriff?" he asked in a hollow, gritty voice.

"Gabriel Miller," Gabe replied carefully, disliking the stranger at once. "Around here, sheriffing ain't a full-time job," he added, after a second glance at the newcomer's gun.

"Seems I remember the cemetery bein' south of town," he said, aiming a look in a southerly direction before his gaze returned to Gabe. "It's been a spell. Maybe you'll know if that's where they buried Johnny Ramsey."

Gabe frowned. "Don't recall any Ramseys from these parts, but I reckon it's possible."

The stranger nodded. "Much obliged, Sheriff. I'll have a look for myself." He touched the brim of his hat in a lazy salute.

"It's south, maybe a quarter mile," Gabe told him, pointing to a hilltop studded with live oaks. "You can't miss it. There'll be a wrought-iron fence needing a coat of paint. You'll see all the markers. This town lost a bunch of sons to the war. Mind if I ask who this Johnny Ramsey was?"

A considerable amount of time passed before the stranger said, "He was my brother." He spoke with an unmistakable edge to his voice, as though the words had a bitter taste. "Never got the chance to pay my respects. I was off to the war with Hood."

Gabe's scowl deepened. "The war's been over better'n ten years."

The newcomer's cheeks turned to stone. "I was delayed," he replied coldly. He lifted his reins, touched a spur to the roan's ribs, and started away from the sheriff's office.

"Say there, stranger!" Gabe called to the rider's back. "I never did catch your name . . ."

A tug on the curb chain stopped the horse. The rider turned in his saddle and cast a level stare at Gabe. "The name's Buck Ramsey," he said menacingly, as though the name itself conveyed some dark threat Gabe should understand. "I aim to find out how my little brother died, so I 'spect I'll have some questions for you later on, Sheriff. Just now, I've got other business."

The roan moved away a second time, striking a jog trot, carrying its rider southeast down Main Street. Gabe watched until the horse trotted past the Broken Spoke Saloon, then by the Culpepper Mercantile, to make a turn due south down the lane to the city cemetery beyond the hill.

"Buck Ramsey," Gabe whispered, certain the name was familiar, although he couldn't remember where he'd heard it before. There weren't any Ramseys around Eagle Springs — he was sure of that. So why did the stranger's name touch something in his memory?

For a half minute more he watched the roan gelding move down the lane until it came to the bottom of the hill. Gabe knew Martha was waiting lunch for him at home, yet he couldn't shake the feeling that the name Buck Ramsey should mean something to him. Maybe he had read it on a Wanted circular from the county seat sometime back?

Frowning, he went back to the office and rummaged through the drawers of the battered rolltop desk. The desk was full of old papers Sheriff Barnes had left behind when he retired the previous winter. Harvey Barnes was dying slowly from consumption and even a part-time job had become too much for him.

Gabe thumbed through yellowed reward posters, some of them dog-eared with age. A lawman in Eagle Springs hardly ever saw the types advertised on the circulars. The town had no bank and only one saloon, not much of interest to desperados on the lookout for easy pickings. When Harvey told Gabe about some of the sheriff's duties around Eagle Springs, he had made a joke of the fact that the county seat sent reward notices there, calling it a waste of time. "The most dangerous part of this job is collectin' back taxes from Widow Hawkins," he said. "She chased me off her front porch with a wet mop one time

. . . back in '72, if I remember right. She claimed she'd paid enough taxes, for no more'n she was gettin' from Coryell County for her money. Dodgin' that mop was about the closest I ever come to gettin' hurt doin' this job. Every now an' then there'll be a rowdy drunk or two down at the Broken Spoke. If you carry a gun while you're wearin' this badge, it'll likely get rusted afore you ever find a need for it."

Gabe came to the bottom of the last drawer and shook his head. No circulars contained Buck Ramsey's name. He sighed and got up from his chair, still nagged by the feeling that he had seen the name somewhere before.

He locked the door again and started homeward, his head bent into a chill wind from the north. Gabe was sure of one thing, as he trudged along. There was something about Ramsey he didn't like. It wasn't just the gun poorly hidden beneath his coat or that he was a stranger to these parts: Some men had a look about them that warned others away, in the same way sighting a rattlesnake made folks choose another direction.

Heading west along a pair of wagon ruts running toward Gatesville that would take him past the rough eighty-acre farm where he raised cotton and corn, Gabe's thoughts focused on Buck Ramsey. The two-mile journey would take him across a ridge a half mile from town, where he would have a distant view of the Eagle Springs cemetery. Most days, he saddled the mule for the trip to the office. But today he had walked, after discovering that the mule had a touch of founder. He didn't mind the journey afoot when weather allowed it, though today he found himself wishing for the mule, which would have given him the chance to ride close to the graveyard while the stranger was there, perhaps to witness his visit unnoticed. He couldn't get his mind off the newcomer and the reason he gave for his return. Gabe had been only nine at the end of the war, Martha just eight. Would she remember a family named Ramsey?

Leaning into the wind, Gabe caught himself looking toward the ridge: If he walked cross-country, he would have a vantage point where he could see the cemetery. A few steps more and he turned up his coat collar before aiming south to walk across an open field that would take him to the base of the ridge. Curiosity was getting the best of him and he cursed himself silently for giving in to the urge.

He crossed the meadow, paying little attention to the whisper of his boots through curls and tufts of winter-dry grass. Beginning the slope, he looked over his shoulder to see if anyone in town might be watching. Not that it mattered all that much. Should anyone ask, he could rightfully claim the walk was official business.

He was short of breath by the time he made the top of the ridge. Looking down on Eagle Springs, he noticed the cotton bales near the gin and thought about how desperately he needed to sell his own cotton. Cotton buyers were making few offers for last fall's crop, what with an oversupply waiting on wharfs at Galveston for shipment to foreign markets. In the decade-long aftermath of the war, cotton farmers seemed to have suffered most. Production exceeded demand. Growing more cotton made no sense except for those who farmed land unsuitable for anything else.

Gabe stopped when he could see the cemetery. He shaded his eyes from the sun. At first it appeared the graveyard was empty, until a shadow moved beneath a live oak tree, the blue roan Buck Ramsey rode to town, tied to a low limb.

Then he caught a glimpse of a man standing between the grave markers with his hat in his hand, his head bowed. Grass had grown knee-high in the cemetery during the summer and no one had taken a scythe to it, making it harder to see anyone inside the fence. Gabe watched from the top of the ridge as a knot began to form in his stomach. He had the feeling Buck Ramsey's visit to the Eagle Springs graveyard bore something far more ominous than he first guessed, remembering something Ramsey said: *I 'spect I'll have some questions for you later on . . .*

"Wonder what he meant by that?" Gabe asked the question aloud, although he was alone on top of the ridge. Frowning, he watched the cold-eyed stranger replace his hat, then turn slowly for his tethered horse. Ramsey mounted his horse and sat quietly for a moment with his face turned toward the grave marker.

The scene taking place below the ridge was like something out of a dream. Gabe tried to imagine what had kept Buck from his brother's final resting place for ten years. What other business could be more important than saying farewell to a brother?

Ramsey reined his horse away from the cemetery fence, then aimed for Eagle Springs; moments later, he rode out of sight.

Gabe swallowed. A curious dryness had come to his throat. A little voice inside his head warned that he shouldn't dally over lunch with Martha. Trouble was brewing in Eagle Springs and he could almost taste it as he hurried off the top of the ridge to head for home.

CHAPTER 2

When he was still a quarter mile from the cabin, their dog saw him and raced off the porch. The old red hound met him halfway, tail wagging. Gabe grinned. "You're gettin' too fat, Red," Gabe said, scratching the dog behind its ears. "Time we cut down on your feed or you'll barely be able to waddle."

Continuing along the road, he caught the scent of food on a gust of wind. Smoke curled from the stovepipe above the kitchen. "Smells like we're havin' fried pork," he told the dog, lengthening his strides as hunger rumbled in his belly. He came to the porch and hurried up the steps. Remembering to pull off his hat before he entered the house, he came in unannounced, smiling when Martha turned away from the cast-iron stove.

"You're late," she said warmly, returning his smile. "The cornbread's been ready almost an hour."

"Something kept me," he told her, hanging his hat and coat on a wooden peg near the door. "Did you ever know of a Ramsey family around Eagle Springs? Ever hear of Johnny Ramsey? Or a brother named Buck?"

Her face showed recognition almost at once. "Johnny Ramsey is the boy who was killed during the war," she said. "He wasn't a soldier — he wasn't old enough. One day Miss Tarver sent someone looking for Johnny when he didn't show up for school. His body was found down by the creek. What made you ask?"

Gabe went to the washbasin and poured just enough water from the tin pitcher to soap his hands. "His brother just rode into town. Said his name was Buck and asked directions to the cemetery. He came to pay his respects."

"I don't remember a brother named Buck," she said thoughtfully, with a glance out the kitchen window. "Why did he wait more than ten years to come back?"

"He didn't really explain," Gabe replied, working a bar of lye soap to lather his hands. "There's something about him makes me worry. I just know I've heard his name somewhere before."

Martha was frowning, and Gabe thought how pretty she looked, even wearing a scowl. Her golden hair caught sunlight from the window, making her braids look like chains of gold. Her eyes were emerald green and sparkled when she smiled. She'd been the prettiest

17

girl at the Eagle Springs school, the reason he had sometimes walked the distance from his home in Leon Junction when his sorrel pony was sorefooted, so he wouldn't miss a chance to court her. Walking twelve miles hardly seemed like anything when his mind was on Martha Elizabeth.

"Maybe you ought to ask Alice about the Ramseys," she said, taking her eyes from the window to spoon peas and pork rind into a bowl. "Alice was about the same age as Johnny. She'll remember more than I do about what happened back then. The day Johnny got killed, his ma came up missing too. Most of their stuff was gone, like Miz Ramsey just packed up and slipped away. That's about all I remember. Everybody was sorry to hear about what happened to Johnny."

"How did Johnny die?" Gabe asked, drying his hands on a cup towel.

Martha gave him a questioning look. "Didn't y'all hear about it in Leon Junction? I thought everybody in the county knew the story, because it was so strange. Folks talked about it for years. He was shot. They found his body down by the creek behind their shack. The Ramseys used to live close to Widow Hawkins . . . that old house where nobody lives now, the one where the roof has fallen in. Nobody remembered hearing a shot.

Miz Hawkins said she didn't hear a thing."

Gabe took a chair at the table, admiring a pan of peach cobbler sitting on a potholder near the middle of a blue-and-white-checked tablecloth covering the rough planks he'd taken from the old cow shed. It wasn't much of a table, but when Martha spread the cloth over it, hiding its crude construction, it looked just fine. He could smell the cinnamon swimming around the piecrust and his mouth began to water. "I don't remember any of it," he said quietly. "Folks at Leon Junction didn't talk about it all that much, I reckon. The only reason I went to Eagle Springs back then was to see a girl named Martha."

She was smiling again when she brought his bowl of peas to the table. She bent down to kiss him, a light peck on the cheek that made him blush. "That girl grew up and was foolish to marry a boy from the Junction," she said. "Everybody in these parts knows that boys from the Junction act plumb crazy when there's a full moon. My ma told me I'd be better off if I married a wooden Indian. She said none of the Miller family had any good sense worth talkin' about. She cried the day I told her I was gonna marry you."

He feigned irritation. "You should have listened to your ma," he told her, lifting his spoon to slurp juice from the black-eyes that

19

were still too hot to eat. "That way, I'd still be single. I could go a-courtin' Miss Peggy Sue Wade if I took the notion. After I got her to marry me, I'd be rich."

"Peggy Sue Wade indeed!" Martha spat, placing her hands on her hips. "You and every other cowboy this side of Waco! You'd have to wait your turn, Gabriel Miller!"

He suppressed a laugh, filling his mouth with the salty pea juice instead. "Where's the cornbread?" he asked, changing the subject as quickly as he could.

Martha pouted. "I ought to feed it to the hogs, after what you said about courting Peggy Sue Wade. Why don't you ask Peggy Sue if she'll bake some for you?"

"What was Johnny Ramsey like?" he asked, suddenly serious again. "Do you remember him?"

Martha gave the cabin wall a blank stare. "He was twelve or so, I think, when he got killed. They were real poor. His pa got killed right after he was born, if I remember right."

Gabe tasted the black-eyed peas, ignoring the burning of his tongue. "How come nobody could figure out who shot him?"

Martha wiped her hands on her apron as she walked back to the stove for the pan of cornbread. "Nearly everybody was gone to the war," she said absently. "About all I remember is what Ma told me about it. Sheriff Barnes asked a whole lot of questions, but he never arrested anyone and nobody ever heard from Miz Ramsey again. Folks used to whisper about it after it happened, tryin' to guess how it all came about. But a while later word started comin' back about all the Eagle Springs soldiers who got killed at Gettysburg and Franklin. Pretty soon, there was plenty of grief to go around and folks forgot all about Johnny Ramsey and his ma."

Gabe took a piece of cornbread when Martha returned to the table, and began to butter it. "If I was to venture a guess, I'd say this Buck Ramsey is on the dodge from the law someplace. He was wearing a gun belt . . . I could see it under his coat."

"Plenty of honest folks carry guns," Martha said, taking a chair opposite Gabe.

"It wasn't just the gun . . . Hard to say just what it was about him that put me to wonderin'. Some men have a certain look about 'em. I can't explain it proper, but it was there just the same."

Martha bit into a piece of cornbread with a thoughtful look on her face. "Maybe you're taking the sheriffing job too serious. I know you've been worried about doing it right, on account of some folks figuring you were too young to wear that badge."

"I got voted this job," he protested, glancing up from his peas. "There were enough folks who believed I could do it to get me elected."

She reached across the table to touch his hand when she heard the tone of his voice. "They trust you," she said reassuringly. "I was only thinking maybe you're worrying too much about Johnny's brother showing up after so long."

"Maybe," he replied. "I didn't like the look of him, and I'd nearly swear I've heard his name before. He rode out to the cemetery, then he headed back toward town."

"Talk to Alice," she said. "She'll remember how it all happened. You could ask Miz Hawkins too. She lived closest to them. Maybe she'll recall that Johnny had a brother."

Gabe nodded. "Miz Hawkins used to do laundry?"

"Until she got too old," Martha replied. "Her husband didn't leave her much. Long as I knew her, she was poor."

"That was back when Eagle Springs could be called a town," Gabe said. "Before so many got killed in the war . . . before cotton got so cheap it broke half the small farmers."

"Like us." Martha sighed. "I wish you could find some better land to farm on shares, Gabe. Cotton ain't worth much, and we can't hardly raise enough corn to feed ourselves."

"Things'll get better," he promised, thinking about the previous year's poor crops. "It has to rain sooner or later. Then we'll plant other things. Tomatoes, maybe. More corn will grow."

"The sheriff money helps," she said. "We'll get by."

Gabe looked across the table at his wife. "I know we will," he told her gently. "We won't be poor all our lives — I promise you that."

She smiled. "Maybe by then we'll have a baby . . . a boy, like you said you wanted."

Her remark embarrassed him a little. Having children was something he rarely talked about. "Nearly every man wants a son, some time or another," he admitted softly, stirring his peas to avoid the look she gave him. "Nothing wrong with that, that I can see."

She touched his hand again. "Nothing at all," she whispered. "Now eat your lunch or you'll be late getting back to town, Sheriff Miller. Don't want you losing that job on account of idle talk. Folks are liable to gossip if you stay too long over the noon hour. They'll wonder what we're up to."

His cheeks colored. "You hadn't oughta talk like that, Martha. It don't seem right, while the sun's still up," he said. "Decent folks wait till it's dark."

He ate the last spoonful of peas, noticing that his wife didn't blush at the suggestion of something naughty. Lately, he'd worried some about how brazen she'd become when it came to private matters. Only last month, she'd taken a bath without turning out the lantern, giving him a glimpse of things he wasn't supposed to see. He'd done his best not to look at her nakedness, only taking a peek now and then through his eyelashes when he was sure she wouldn't notice.

As he got up from the table, she said playfully, "Nothing wrong about it, day or night, not between folks who're married. Only one way I know of to make a baby." She smiled slyly. "Besides, sometimes at night, you drop right off to sleep, 'specially after you've been plowing. You used to be real romantic soon as the sun went down."

He took his bowl to the washtub, wishing she wouldn't talk about personal things quite so frankly. "Plowing's hard work," he protested, hoping she would drop the subject. "You oughta know that . . ."

He heard her giggle as he was turning around.

"When we first got married, I didn't notice you bein' all that tired after a day in the fields," she said, teasing him wickedly.

He sighed and shook his head. "This ain't

a very ladylike thing for you to be talking about, Martha. If your ma could hear you just now, she'd throw a walleyed fit and make you go to church twice on Sundays."

"She wouldn't!" Martha argued, still sounding playful. "She's the one who told me all about having babies, and she never said a woman had to get pregnant in the dark."

To escape any further discussion, he headed for the wall peg to fetch his coat and hat. "I've got papers to serve this afternoon," he told her. "The Cummingses haven't paid their county taxes and Judge Green sent over the notice. I'm sorta dreading having to serve Clarence with it. He worked as hard as anybody last year. It ain't his fault cotton won't sell this winter."

Martha stood up when she saw him sleeve into his coat. "There's liable to be a bunch of folks owing back taxes around here," she said, coming toward him, her smile gone now. "We could be in the same shape if it wasn't for your job in town. I feel sorry for the Cummingses, all those mouths they've got to feed and poor Miz Cummings expecting again." She stood on her toes to kiss him as he was putting on his hat. "Makes me wonder if we hadn't oughta wait a spell to have a baby," she added, concern darkening her face, "until we see if our own cotton fetches a price."

It was something he'd worried about lately, too, when no cotton buyers showed up at the gin to make offers. Tons of unsold cotton sat in the gin yards at Waco, he'd been told. It could be argued that this year cotton wasn't worth anything. "The price will come up sooner or later," he said with an assurance he didn't really feel. "It always has. Folks have got to wear clothes . . . can't go naked."

At that, Martha tilted her face and her smile returned. "They could . . . ," she said, batting her eyelashes the way she did when she was feeling naughty.

He could feel his cheeks coloring again.

CHAPTER 3

During the walk back to town, he considered the things Martha had told him about the Ramsey family. Gabe wondered how much Sheriff Barnes would remember about the incident. Harvey's illness kept him bedridden now and there were times when his memory wasn't too good. But talking to Harvey was a starting place to find out more about what happened back then. Then he would talk to Alice Warner. Talking to the Widow Hawkins might help, if she remembered events that far back.

Clara Hawkins was rumored to be crazy now, if town gossip could be believed. Hardly anyone ever visited the old woman. She made infrequent trips to the mercantile and occasional visits to Huffman's General Store for staples such as flour and sugar. She tended a garden behind her house and, for the most part, kept to herself. Some folks held a low opinion of Widow Hawkins; Gabe always assumed it was because of her previous occupation as a laundress, back when Eagle Springs was big enough to need someone who did public laundry.

As he approached the ridge with a view of the cemetery, he turned east, deciding to take a look at the grave marker where Johnny Ramsey was buried. Leaning into the wind, Gabe marched across the ridge, then down its crest toward the cemetery, all the while remembering the face of the new arrival to Eagle Springs, his pale eyes, the gun tied around his waist. Gabe was sure he could smell trouble on the wind as he walked down the slope leading to the rusting iron fence around the burial ground.

He entered the cemetery through a sagging gate that creaked on seldom-used hinges. His boots whispered among tufts of unmown grass as he read the legends on the markers. Dozens of graves had bunches of wilted summer flowers lying near the headstones, most with only a few petals clinging to the brittle stems, proof that someone still mourned a loved one's passing.

Near a corner of the fence, where uncut grass stood tallest, he found the name Johnny Ramsey enscribed on a small piece of weathered stone. The dates 1852–1864 appeared below the name. The marker contained no mention of relatives or any other information.

Gabe shoved his hands in his coat pockets. The walk to the cemetery had been a waste of time.

"I'll talk to Harvey," he said, casting a glance downhill to the outskirts of town where a cabin built from post oak logs sat near the gin. Harvey hadn't been seen in town lately and word was that the consumption would claim him soon. During the summer, he'd come to the Broken Spoke a few times, using a pair of walking sticks and coughing up blood from the exertion. He'd been a good rancher and a tough lawman, according to those who knew him before the war. He'd been too old to go off to fight Yankees when the war started, having a touch of rheumatism by then.

At the bottom of the hill Gabe lengthened his stride when he caught a glimpse of a saddled horse tied to the hitchrail in front of the Broken Spoke. Even from a distance he recognized the rawboned blue gelding and wondered what Ramsey was doing at the town saloon. "Asking questions," Gabe told himself under his breath, hurrying toward Main Street. "Carl wasn't here during the war." The bartender was unlikely to have the answers Ramsey wanted, having gone to war the same as most of the fighting-age men around the county back then.

Close to Main, Gabe glanced at the shack

belonging to Clara Hawkins. Her house sat on the banks of the creek where, before the war, she had drawn water for the public laundry. There were still heaps of ashes behind her house, where she had tended her boiling kettles. Two hundred yards farther east, the crumbling walls of the old house where Martha said the Ramsey family used to live stood stark and empty, overgrown with gourd vines and brush. Behind what was left of the house, a ramshackle livestock shed leaned crookedly above the creekbank. When Gabe saw the shed, he wondered if that might be where Johnny Ramsey had met his end.

Gabe turned for the saloon when he struck Main Street, one eye on the roan horse, the bedroll, and war bag tied to the saddle. By the look of Ramsey's traveling gear, he'd come some distance to reach Eagle Springs.

He climbed the boardwalk in front of the Broken Spoke and walked to the batwing doors. Despite the winter chill, Carl usually left the solid oak doors open, heating the place with a big potbelly stove during cold months. Carl Jones had bought the drinking establishment from Herman Whitaker's widow right after the war. Herman had lost his life at Gettysburg. So many men from Eagle Springs didn't come back from the war, which was one reason the town had dwindled down after the collapse of the Confederacy in '65.

Gabe shouldered through the batwings, out of breath from the long walk back to town. He spotted a lone patron at the bar and knew the man's identity without waiting for his eyes to adjust to the poor light in the saloon. Carl was standing near Ramsey, making idle swipes across the bar with a rag. Carl looked up as soon as Gabe started across the floor. Buck Ramsey had been watching from the moment Gabe entered the place. Gabe noticed that Ramsey's right hand hung near the butt of his pistol, the tail of his duster tucked behind a holster tied low on his right leg.

"Howdy, Gabe," Carl said, nodding once. Then he aimed a thumb at Ramsey. "Got a feller here who's been askin' about what happened to his brother. You ever hear of a kid by the name of Johnny Ramsey?"

Gabe approached the bar, trying to read Buck Ramsey's face in the shadow below his hat brim. "I already told this stranger I never heard of a Ramsey family around here. We've met," he added, inclining his head toward Buck.

"This here's our sheriff," Carl said, addressing Ramsey. "He's a bit on the young side, maybe, but he does the job right well."

Ramsey's eyes moved up and down Gabe's frame. There was no friendliness in his stare.

"I can see he's young," Ramsey said, speaking in the same gravelly voice he had used before. "Somebody around here will remember what happened to my brother. I'll keep askin'. I've got plenty of time."

"My wife remembers Johnny," Gabe said. "I asked her about him at lunch. She said someone found him down at the creek behind the house where they used to live. Somebody shot him . . . nobody ever figured out who did it. Your ma left that same day, according to my wife. Nobody knew where she went, or why she left so sudden-like when your brother died."

Ramsey stiffened. "Who was sheriff back then?" he asked coldly, his eyes boring holes through Gabe.

Gabe swallowed as an uncomfortable dryness entered his mouth. "A man by the name of Harvey Barnes. He's dying of the consumption. Can't hardly get out of bed anymore."

"Where does he live?" Ramsey asked. "I need directions to his house."

Gabe glanced at Carl, then back to Ramsey. Harvey was too sick to want company. "Northwest of the gin," Gabe replied, "but I wouldn't advise you to go. I said he was dying . . ."

Ramsey's eyelids narrowed a little. "When I want advice from you, I'll ask for it," he

32

said, his voice like a rasp across cold iron. "He'll talk to me. Somebody around here's gonna give me some answers."

Gabe was left without choices. He couldn't ignore Ramsey's challenge. "I said Harvey's sick."

"I'll be the judge of that," Ramsey said, straightening up from the bar. "It ain't likely he's too sick to answer a couple of questions."

"It's my job to investigate that sort of thing," Gabe answered, hooking his thumbs in the front pockets of his denims, hoping to end it. "I'll find out everything you need to know . . . everything Harvey remembers. Be glad to tell you what he says."

The muscles in Ramsey's cheeks turned hard. "Maybe you didn't hear me the first time, son. I aim to ask this Harvey Barnes a few questions myself. Don't push me on it. I rode a hell of a long way to find out what happened to my brother."

It went against Gabe's nature not to have the last word, not when he represented the law in Eagle Springs. "I said I'd talk to him and that's the way it's gonna be," he said, rocking back on his boot heels. "Harvey's dying. His wife don't want him disturbed."

Ramsey squared himself in front of Gabe. He was several inches taller, heavier by as much as fifty pounds, but it wasn't his weight or his height that worried Gabe. The gun he wore strapped to his leg was reason for caution.

"I don't figure you'll try to stop me," Ramsey said hoarsely, glaring down at Gabe. "No sense in gettin' yourself killed over a few questions."

"Are you threatening me?" Gabe asked, determined that he wouldn't be ignored. He'd known all along that a time might come when the badge he wore would put him in a tight spot. He looked down at Ramsey's gun. "I'm not armed, but I won't stand aside if you head over to Harvey's place. I'll have to try to stop you."

Ramsey watched him for a moment before he spoke again. Carl was frozen behind the bar, the dishrag motionless as he listened to what was being said.

"You could be buyin' yourself a grave up yonder near my little brother," he said quietly. "Crossing me would be a mistake."

"Maybe," Gabe replied, trying to keep his fear from showing. "I reckon that's a chance I'll have to take. If Harvey's well enough to talk to you, I'll send word. Otherwise, I'm ordering you to stay clear of his place. If he can tell me anything you need to know, I'll tell you what he said."

There was a lingering silence as Ramsey

looked at Gabe with pure hatred in his eyes. Then his expression changed slowly to mild irritation. "You're either awful dumb, or you've got more guts than sense. This time, I won't call your bluff — if you're bluffing like I figure you are. Ask the old man if he'll see me."

"I'll ask," Gabe said, as he started to turn for the door. Then he stopped and looked over his shoulder. "By the way, Mr. Ramsey, I wasn't bluffing. Never was much good at lying. You've got my word that I'll do everything I can to get to the bottom of what happened to your brother. He died before my time, but there'll be folks who remember it. I'll let you know what I find out."

Without waiting for Ramsey to say more, he walked to the batwings, then out on the boardwalk. A gust of wind struck him full in the face as he started for Harvey's house behind the gin. Along the way, he thought about the moment when he faced Buck Ramsey's threat without a gun. Judging by his looks, Ramsey possessed too much skill with a pistol for Gabe to stand a chance against him in a face-off. Should it come down to the business of guns, Gabe needed an advantage, and the odds would still be against him.

Passing the gin, he hardly looked at the bales of cotton stacked in neat rows across the yard.

Preoccupied with guessing at the circumstances leading to a twelve-year-old boy's death from a gunshot, he also considered what the sudden disappearance of the boy's mother meant. Had she left town hurriedly as soon as her son was killed? Or did she leave in the middle of some sort of disturbance that finally cost young Johnny his life? The best source of information about the affair was Harvey, if Harvey wasn't too sick to talk, if his memory was still clear for an event a decade earlier. It was the logical starting place, to find out what was officially known about the matter.

He came to the porch at Harvey's house, climbed the stairs, and knocked gently. A half minute later, Harvey's wife, Bernice, answered his knock. She recognized him at once and waved him in.

"How are you, Gabriel?" she asked warmly. "I suppose you came to see Harvey . . ."

"If he's feeling okay, ma'am," he replied. "Just need to ask him a question or two."

She motioned him to a bedroom door. "He's awake," she said after a glance through the opening. "Go right in. He's always so glad to see you."

Gabe entered the bedroom with his hat in his hands. Lying atop a four-poster bed, the old man beneath the bed covers was hardly recognizable. His eyes were the same, but the rest of his face had become gaunt and colorless. Gabe smiled. "How've you been?" he asked, saying it softly.

Harvey grinned weakly. "Not too bad fer a dyin' man," he answered. "How's the job?"

"Okay, I reckon. There's a stranger in town, asking about his dead brother. It happened before my time, so I figured I'd better ask you about it."

Harvey scowled. "What's his name? How long ago — ?"

"The stranger gave his name as Buck Ramsey. Johnny Ramsey was his brother. I just had a look at the grave."

He could tell by the look on Harvey's face that he remembered it. Harvey pinched his eyebrows again, this time with a worried look. "Buck Ramsey is here? Askin' about Johnny?"

Gabe nodded. "Just rode in about noon. I asked him why he took so long, coming to visit his brother's grave. All he said was that he'd been delayed."

"Buck Ramsey." Harvey said the name again, softer now. "Be careful when you're around Buck. You know about him, I reckon."

"Not exactly," Gabe replied. "The name did sound on the familiar side."

"It oughta be," Harvey whispered. "He's a dangerous man. They called his kind a shootist, back in my time. Same as a gunfighter.

A paid gun is what he is. A killer for hire. Last I heard of Buck, he was doin' a stretch in Yuma prison. Appears he's done his time . . ."

"He wants to know how his brother died," Gabe said. "How much do you remember?"

Harvey's gaze wandered to a bedroom window as Gabe thought about Buck. Ramsey was a hired gun; the Yuma prison sentence explained why it took him ten years to make it back to Eagle Springs.

"We found the boy one morning, back in '64, I believe it was, early in the spring. April maybe. He had a bullet hole in his chest." Harvey spoke slowly, as though the memory of that day pained him. "The house was half empty, most of the closets bare. Their old mule and buckboard were gone, along with Anna Ramsey, the boy's mother. Nobody could figure why Anna wasn't there, why she'd cleared out, whether she left before or after the boy was killed. None of it made any sense. Why would the woman leave without telling us what happened? And if he wasn't dead when she left, why did she run out on a twelve-year-old boy and never try to find him again? Whoever shot the boy didn't leave any clues behind. No footprints, just them tracks the wagon made when Anna drove off. The wagon was headed northwest; I followed the tracks until I lost them down at Beaver

Draw in all them rocks. I looked all over fer a couple of days . . . never found no trace of that wagon's tracks."

Gabe remembered something Martha had told him. "I was wondering if Miz Hawkins had any idea who done it, living so close the way she does. Looks like she'd have heard the gun go off, unless she was hard of hearing back then, same as now."

Harvey spread his palms helplessly. Gabe noticed that his hands were trembling slightly and he wondered if it might be caused by the consumption.

"I talked to Clara," Harvey remembered. "She swore an oath she didn't hear a damn thing that night, or the day before, either. Worst case I ever had the whole time I was sheriff and I couldn't solve it. Hell, I'd almost forgotten about it, till you mentioned that Buck was here." He looked closely at Gabe. "You be careful around that Buck Ramsey, Gabriel. Time was, right after the war was over, he was a wanted man in two or three states an' maybe some of the Territories. He rode with Quantrill for a spell. He was nothin' but a damned outlaw until the law caught up with him near Fort Grant."

"He wants to talk to you about what happened to Johnny," Gabe said. "He's got some question . . ."

39

The old man turned even paler than before. He looked at Gabe, blinked, and said, "I'll see him. Send him out. I figure he deserves some answers."

CHAPTER 4

The walk back to the Broken Spoke provided an opportunity for Gabe to do some thinking. Harvey had seemed worried, not only by the fact that Buck Ramsey was in town, but also by the prospect of meeting him face to face. It wasn't like Harvey to appear anxious. Did Harvey know more about Johnny Ramsey's death than he was willing to tell? Or was it simply Buck's reputation that made Harvey edgy?

Learning that Buck had been one of Quantrill's raiders was something of a surprise. Long after the war, folks talked about Quantrill's exploits in Texas after being hounded out of Missouri by Union patrols. Gabe remembered his father's low opinion of Quantrill's bunch, calling them nothing but murderers and thieves. Splinter factions looted across parts of Texas long after the war ended. Hardly a week passed without mention in the Waco newspaper of remnants of Quantrill's gang, until the last of them were rounded up.

Gabe supposed Buck Ramsey could fit the description of a cold-blooded killer and thief and had been a part of the bunch hunted down by the law at the close of the war. Gabe wondered, though, if he was making that assumption because of what Harvey told him.

Gabe approached the saloon, noting that Ramsey's horse was still tied out front. Knowing about Ramsey's reputation made him uneasy about their next meeting. Gabe knew he'd been right when he smelled trouble on the wind earlier in the day. Having a convicted killer prowling the countryside was enough to make any lawman nervous.

He walked into the Broken Spoke to find Ramsey idling over a shot of whiskey. Ramsey watched him from the moment he entered the place; the gunman evidenced unusual caution when Gabe was around. It figured he was similarly cautious when anyone approached him. Gabe wondered if he should have gone to the office first to pick up his gun, though he reasoned that he was no match for Ramsey with a sidearm. It was far better to handle matters peacefully, if Ramsey would allow it.

"I talked to Harvey," he said, halting a few feet away from the bar where Ramsey stood. "He told me everything he remembers. He said he'd talk to you, only his wife asked that we don't stay too long. Harvey's been real weak lately."

The gunman shook his head. He downed his drink without saying a word, then tossed a silver coin on the bar. "Lead the way," he said as he closed the front of his duster over his gun.

Gabe wheeled for the door. "Harvey knows who you are," he said quietly when Ramsey came up beside him. "He told me you'd been in prison, so I reckon that explains why you took so long getting here."

Ramsey gave him a disinterested look as they went through the batwings. "I did my time," he replied without emotion.

"Harvey told me you rode with Quantrill," Gabe added, turning down the boardwalk.

Ramsey grunted. His stare turned icy. "It's none of his affair who I rode with. I haven't broken any laws in this town."

"Never said you had," Gabe told him, walking slowly along the boards. "I only mentioned it . . . what Harvey said about you." He stopped at the end of the boardwalk before making the turn toward Harvey's house. He looked Ramsey in the eye. "Look, Mr. Ramsey, I'm doing everything I can to help you find out what happened to your brother. There's no call to be so touchy. I know you've got a mean reputation, but you ain't gonna scare me with tough talk. I'm trying to help you."

The gunman was silent a moment. His eyes never left Gabe's face. "I get touchy when some gent pokes his nose into affairs that ain't his. The stretch I did at Yuma has got nothing to do with my bein' here. I make no secret of the fact I rode with Quantrill during the war. I was with Bloody Bill Anderson for a spell after Quantrill was wounded. You're too young to understand what that war was like, so don't judge me. You weren't there."

Gabe shrugged. "My pa went. He told me about it. He was one of the lucky ones to make it back home. I wasn't poking my nose into your past . . . I was telling you what Harvey said, about the reason you got delayed."

Finally Ramsey looked elsewhere, to the horizon. "I've had a lot of time to wonder about what happened to my family," he said in a faraway voice. "The trail starts here, where my brother died. It'd take a yellow son of a bitch to shoot a twelve-year-old boy. When I find out who did it, I'm gonna kill him."

By the way Ramsey said it, Gabe knew he meant to keep his word. "We may not ever know who shot him," Gabe remarked. "That was a long time ago, plenty of time for the killer to disappear."

"Maybe," Ramsey whispered, still watching

the horizon. "I don't give up easy."

Gabe stepped off the boardwalk, aiming for Harvey's house. The gunman followed, his spurs rattling over the hard-packed dirt road. Gabe thought about what Ramsey said. Ramsey made it plain that he meant to stay in Eagle Springs until he found his brother's killer, and Gabe knew things wouldn't be the same in this part of the county until Ramsey was satisfied.

They came to Harvey's porch. Gabe knocked on the door, sorting through what little information he had concerning the death of Johnny Ramsey. It was almost nothing, and all of it had taken place ten years ago.

Bernice opened the door a crack, then she smiled at Gabe and let them in. "He's waiting for you," she said. She looked at Ramsey briefly. "I hope you won't upset him. He'll start coughing, and lately he's been spitting up so much blood."

"We won't stay long," Gabe promised, remembering to pull off his hat. He led the way to the bedroom door, knowing the sound of Ramsey's spurs would alert Harvey to their arrival.

Harvey was propped up on pillows when they entered the room. He merely nodded to Gabe as he watched Ramsey approach the bed. "I'm Harvey Barnes," he said, addressing the gunman in a phlegmy voice.

Ramsey inclined his head. "The boy tells me you know who I am and why I'm here," he began, looking down at the bed with no friendliness.

Gabe turned to Ramsey. "I'd be obliged if you stopped calling me a boy. I'm old enough to hold down the sheriff's job. Most folks call me Gabe."

Ramsey seemed irritated. He shrugged slightly, as if to say it didn't matter, and said to Harvey, "Tell me what you remember, the day they found Johnny. Don't leave anything out."

Harvey's frail hands caught the edge of his quilt, knotting, and Gabe was sure he saw a tiny tremor in Harvey's fingers. For a moment, Harvey stared at the ceiling.

"I don't remember who came to the office to tell me about findin' the body," Harvey began. "A widow by the name of Clara Hawkins lived close by and she probably sent somebody. I hurried down to the creek. Johnny was lyin' on his back. There was an old shotgun beside him . . . hadn't been fired. Appeared he dropped it when he got shot. There was a bullet hole in his chest. Blood all over the ground. I judged the hole was made by a big-bore gun, a .44 maybe. I reckon it was around nine in the morning when I got there. That pool of blood around him was might' near dry, so I figured he was killed early the night before."

A wet, rattling sound had begun in Harvey's chest as he was talking. He paused and raised a hand to his mouth, then coughed up a mouthful of bloody spittle, wincing in pain. He wiped his hand on a towel lying atop the quilt and stared at the ceiling again. "The house was empty. Your ma was gone, and so was her old wagon and the mule she kept down at the shed. Hardly any clothes left in the wardrobe closets, like your ma took everything with her. Nobody saw her leave town or heard the wagon. There was tracks leadin' across the creek. I followed those wheel prints on horseback until they crossed a stretch of rock at a place called Beaver Draw, northwest of town. I scouted around and couldn't find no trace of the wagon after that, like it just up an' disappeared. That was the end of it.

"We buried Johnny the next day. I sent a letter to you, in care of Hood's First Texas Cavalry, tellin' what happened. Somebody remembered that you'd joined up with Hood's Brigades when the war started. Got a letter back nearly a year later, sayin' you wasn't with Hood anymore. Some colonel with Hood's outfit wrote back that you'd joined Quantrill's guerillas up in Missouri. That's the last we heard of you, until all them Wanted notices

47

started showin' up, claimin' you were with Bloody Bill in Texas."

Another spasm of coughing shook Harvey's chest. With his eyes tightly shut, he coughed more blood into the towel. It was then that Bernice hurried into the bedroom with a worried look on her face.

"That'll have to be enough for today, gentlemen," she said, taking the cloth to wipe the edges of Harvey's mouth. "You can come back tomorrow when he's feeling better, if you feel you simply must talk to him again."

Gabe turned around, keeping an eye on Ramsey. "Let's go," he said softly, when the gunman made no move to leave the room.

"Just one more question," Ramsey insisted. "What did the woman have to say? You said her name was Clara Hawkins . . ."

Harvey shook his head. "She claimed she didn't hear a thing, or see anybody that night," he said, in a voice so thin it was difficult to hear. "She's been a touch on the deaf side for as far back as I can remember."

Something about Ramsey's expression changed. "Maybe she's lyin'," he whispered, then he wheeled away from the bed and walked heavily to the door with his hands shoved deeply into the pockets of his coat. He halted at the door and spoke to Harvey. "I may come back tomorrow," he said, looking across the room. "A whole bunch of things don't add up."

As soon as they were out on the front porch, Ramsey turned to Gabe. "Show me where the woman lives," he said tonelessly.

Gabe glanced across town, past the rooftops to the cutbank where Justin Creek meandered south of the business district. For reasons he couldn't explain just then, he remembered being told that the stream had been named after a cow thief named Justin Lee who was hanged by a vigilante mob of irate citizens from the limb of a giant live oak where the springs flowed into the creek bed. "Some folks around here say she's crazy," Gabe said. "I doubt she'll be able to tell you much. She's deaf as a stone now. You'll have to yell your head off if you want her to hear you."

Now Ramsey looked in the same direction. "She may be the only one who really knows what happened that night. She could have been scared to tell the truth about what she saw or heard."

"It ain't likely," Gabe offered, "but I reckon it's a place to start." He stepped off the porch, expecting Ramsey to follow, but when the gunman's spurs were silent, Gabe turned around.

Ramsey was staring at a cloud of dust coming toward Eagle Springs from the north. Gabe saw the source of the dust and started to explain. "That's Cleveland Wade's carriage, headed to Huffman's to buy supplies, I reckon. He's the richest man in the whole county. Runs cows on twenty sections of the best grazing land in the Leon River bottom. He's got a pretty daughter — her name is Peggy Sue. Darn near every marrying-age man between here and Waco has his eye on her. She's a real beauty."

They watched the sleek black carriage roll closer to town, its canopy layered with chalky dust.

"Fancy rig," Ramsey muttered, frowning some. "I don't recall hearing his name before I left for the war."

"Seems I was told he came here right after the war got started," Gabe remembered. "He bought up a lot of land and set in to ranching. Maybe that's why you don't know the name — you left before Cleve got here."

"You say he has a daughter?" Ramsey asked offhandedly.

"Prettiest girl in the whole county, 'cept for my Martha," Gabe replied, being quick to put Martha at the top of the list even though she couldn't hear him.

Ramsey grunted, then followed Gabe off the porch toward the south side of town, narrowing his eyes when he met a gust of wind carrying dust.

CHAPTER 5

The widow's house was a crude clapboard affair. Weathered boards, long without a coat of paint, gave the place a neglected look. A few vines, dead in winter, clung to trellises covering the windows that helped keep out the sun's glare in summer. An overgrown garden plot sat behind the house. A scarecrow, looking forlorn without a sufficient amount of straw stuffed into the sleeves of a badly worn work shirt, flapped its slender arms in the winter wind at a corner of the garden. The scarecrow's face had been painted on a pillowcase long ago and now its eyes, nose, and mouth were mere smudges, having endured years of weather, unrelenting summer suns and bitterly cold winters often seasoned with weeks of soaking rains. Two hundred yards to the southeast, perched atop the cutbank above Justin Creek, sat the remains of the Ramsey home.

When Buck Ramsey caught a glimpse of the crumbling walls, his footsteps slowed.

51

"That was your place," Gabe said, aiming a finger.

"I hardly remember it," Ramsey told him, still looking at what was left of the house. "We didn't live here but a year or so before the conscription order came. We moved here after my pa died. I didn't like the idea of leavin' Ma and Johnny alone."

"Nobody can figure where your ma went," Gabe said thoughtfully, continuing toward Clara Hawkins's front door. "She just up and vanished that day. For me, that's the hardest thing to figure out. Why would your ma leave so sudden, without telling a soul what happened to Johnny? If I knew the answer to that, why she pulled out without a word the way she did, I bet I'd be a whole lot closer to knowing who shot your brother."

"It wouldn't be like her to just disappear," Ramsey said. "Only thing I've got is a guess. If she got to grievin' over what happened to Johnny . . ." He didn't finish the remark.

"If I could only figure out where she went. Harvey said her clothes were gone from the house. I say that means she wasn't planning on coming back."

Ramsey offered no opinion as they walked to the widow's front door. Gabe climbed a set of sagging wooden steps to knock.

"Seems like I remember this house now,"

Ramsey said, looking downstream, his brow pinched.

Gabe banged on the door. "Hope she hears us," he said, listening for a sound inside. He pounded on the door again, harder this time, then heard the tap of a walking stick on a wood floor. A latch rattled, and when the door opened, Clara Hawkins looked out, blinking in the bright sunlight.

"Afternoon, Miz Hawkins," Gabe said, almost shouting. "Can you spare a minute or two?"

She regarded both men with suspicion. "I suppose," she replied, absently spreading wrinkles from the front of her faded green dress while resting most of her weight on her cane. "What do you want with me?" She answered loudly, as though Gabe and the stranger had the hearing difficulty.

"I want to ask you about the time Johnny Ramsey was killed," Gabe went on, raising his voice. "This is Johnny's brother. His name is Buck, and he's trying to find out how it happened."

The old woman's eyes went quickly to Ramsey, and Gabe could have sworn she looked frightened for a moment. She lifted a liver-spotted hand to her face, brushed a stray lock of silver hair from her forehead. Crow's-feet deepened around her eyes, then relaxed.

"I don't remember much about it," she said, speaking softer now, her gaze flickering from Ramsey to Gabe. "That was a long time ago, and just lately my memory isn't all that good."

Gabe sensed her growing uneasiness. "Are you the one who found him that morning?" he asked.

Clara seemed a bit unsteady on her walking stick just then. She took a moment to answer. "Can't say as I rightly recall," she said. "That was such a long time back. I'm almost eighty years old, you know."

"It might help to know who found him first," Gabe continued, puzzled by the woman's behavior. He was sure she knew more than she was willing to say, although he couldn't guess why, or what it was that made him feel she was hiding something.

"Did you ask Harvey about it?" she inquired. "He's the one who should know . . ."

"We already spoke to Harvey. He wasn't certain who found the body that morning." It might have been Gabe's imagination, but it appeared Clara wouldn't look at Ramsey now.

"Perhaps I did find him," she said, saying it with care. "I don't see how it makes a difference. He was lying down by the creek. Merciful heavens! I remember there was so much blood!"

"Was anybody else there when you found him?" Gabe asked. He was certain the question brought more worry to the woman's face the minute he said it.

"I don't recall," she replied, perhaps a bit too quickly. "I do remember hurrying to the house, looking for the boy's mother. She wasn't there. I suppose Harvey told you that."

"Yes, ma'am, he told us," Gabe agreed. "He also said you didn't hear a gunshot, or the wagon leaving."

"I didn't hear a thing," she told him with emphasis, still unwilling to look at Ramsey. "I've been going deaf for a number of years, young man, and I've always been a sound sleeper."

Gabe looked down at his boots, thinking of more questions, nagged by the feeling Clara knew things she wasn't willing to talk about. "It would be a help if you could remember more," he said. "The murder never was solved, and I've promised Mr. Ramsey that I'd look into it."

Only then did Clara look past Gabe to Buck Ramsey, albeit fleetingly. "I hardly recall the boy had an older brother. It was wartime . . . so many of our young men were gone to fight the Yankees."

"Yes, ma'am," Gabe said as a blast of chilly wind swept across the steps. "Johnny's brother was off to the war when it happened. I figure I owe it to him to do everything I can to investigate the matter."

"Harvey looked into it," Clara remembered. "He couldn't find a trace of the Ramsey woman after she left, or any clues as to who might have killed the boy. I'm quite sure Harvey did the best he could." She shivered from the cold. "I've told you everything I recall about it. Now if you'll excuse me, I think I'll lie down for a spell. Good afternoon, Gabriel. Good afternoon, Mr. Ramsey."

She closed the door before Gabe could think of anything else to ask. He listened to the tap of her cane until the sound grew softer, then turned to Ramsey. "She didn't tell us much we didn't already know," he said.

Ramsey's eyes appeared clouded. "I figure she knows more," he replied in the monotone voice that was beginning to grate on Gabe's nerves.

"Could be," Gabe remarked, coming down the steps. "Trouble is, I don't see any way to get her to talk about it." He looked Ramsey in the eye. "I got the same feeling, that maybe there's more to the story. She appeared to have trouble with a couple of my questions. Can't say for sure . . ."

Ramsey turned, facing the ruins of the shack where he used to live. Wind rustled the tails of his coat, outlining his gaunt frame while he stared at what was left of the house. "I'd give a gambler long odds she knows what happened over yonder," he said quietly, squinting in the sun's glare despite the shade from his hat brim. "Sooner or later, I'll find out what went on that night."

"How?" Gabe asked, scuffing the ground absently with the toe of his boot. "We've talked to darn near everybody who'll remember back that far . . ."

Ramsey didn't answer him for some time, letting his eyes roam up and down the creekbank. "Maybe there's somebody else who saw it," he said later. "I don't aim to leave until I've got what I came for. Somebody'll talk."

Gabe sat at the table, watching Martha prepare their supper, toying with a china cup. Thinking about the day's events, he'd let his coffee turn cold. "That Buck Ramsey is one of the hardest gents I ever came across," he told her absently, remembering Ramsey's actions. "It's real easy to believe he's a killer. He don't hardly ever get agitated. Stares holes plumb through whoever he's looking at. I just know there's gonna be trouble around here before he's done."

"Did you ask Alice about it?" Martha reminded, taking a pan of biscuits from the oven.

"Didn't have the time," he said. "We talked to Harvey, and Miz Hawkins. It was getting late by the time we got through looking around down at the creek. Had to come home to get chores done."

"Alice was Johnny's age. She knew him better'n most. I remember he was real quiet. Hardly ever said a word at school."

"I'll talk to her tomorrow. I got the feeling while we were talking to Miz Hawkins that she knows more than she's telling. She acted like some of the questions made her nervous. Maybe it was only my imagination."

"When is the older brother coming back?" she asked. "Did he say?"

"He's still here," Gabe remembered. "He said he wasn't leaving until he got what he wanted. He's got his mind made up to stay around Eagle Springs until he knows who shot his brother and what came of his ma. He could be here till doomsday."

Martha frowned as she was taking the biscuits from the pan. "Where is he staying? There aren't any rooms for hire."

"He pitched a tent down by the creek. It's just a little one, the kind the army uses."

"Word will spread all over the county," Martha said. "It'll give everybody something to gossip about, that a famous outlaw is camped here, looking for whoever killed his brother."

Gabe nodded. "Anna Ramsey is the key to it," he said thoughtfully. "I've got a feeling that finding out what happened to her unlocks the mystery. She had to know what went on that night. Any fool can see that's why she left in such a hurry, without saying a word to anybody about where she was headed."

"What did Harvey say about her?" Martha asked, bringing the biscuits to the table in a wicker basket covered by a linen napkin.

"He said he followed the wagon tracks up to Beaver Draw, and that's where he lost them. It's mostly rock. To tell the truth, Harvey acted edgy when Buck Ramsey showed up. Harvey's hands were shaking while Ramsey asked questions. It made me wonder if maybe Harvey knows more than he's telling. He behaved real strange, if you ask me."

"Why would he hide anything?" she asked, sitting down across from Gabe.

"I can't figure why," Gabe told her, buttering a biscuit, his mind on the meeting with Harvey. "Like I told you, I got the same feeling when we talked to Clara Hawkins, like there's something about it nobody wants to remember."

"Maybe Alice will know. She was always the nosy kind. One time she asked me if we made love with the lantern lit . . . if I let you see me naked."

He took the plate of chicken and dumplings she handed him and set it down, inhaling the delicious smell. "What did you tell her?" he asked quickly, hoping he wouldn't be embarrassed the next time he saw Alice Warner in town.

"I told her it was none of her business what we did when the lantern was lit. I told her that if I wanted to parade around naked in front of my own husband, I could do it whenever I wanted."

"All you had to say was no," he said. "Now she'll think we never wear any clothes when we're alone. She'll tell everyone in this end of the county that we're naked half the time, and when word gets back to your ma and pa, they'll throw a fit over it."

At that, Martha giggled. "It'll serve 'em right," she said. "Ma's always asking if you treat me nice, like she figured you wouldn't."

He gave up on further discussion about it and started in on his supper, all the while wondering what it was that Harvey and Clara seemed nervous about. The fact that it was wintertime allowed him the chance to look into it further. If Buck Ramsey had shown up in the spring, he'd have been too busy plowing to make many inquiries.

"What does Johnny's brother look like?" Martha asked, watching him across the table.

Gabe thought a minute. "I reckon he's about the meanest looking feller I ever saw. You can tell by the way he handles himself that he's nobody's fool. He warned me that he'd kill the man who shot his brother, soon as he finds out who done it. Can't say as I ever heard a promise I believed any stronger. He means every word of what he said."

Martha stared at him silently for some time, frozen in her chair by what Gabe told her. "Folks will expect the sheriff to try to stop him," she said. "They'll want the killer put in jail, won't they?"

"I 'spect they will, if Ramsey finds out who done it," he replied.

"What will you do, Gabe?"

He didn't want to worry her. "I don't think we'll ever know who shot Johnny. The killer has had ten long years to cover his tracks."

CHAPTER 6

He fed the hogs before daylight and milked the old jersey just as dawn grayed the eastern sky, shivering a little in the predawn chill. He went about the chores early when he found he couldn't sleep soundly during the night. His dreams centered around the arrival of the outlaw in Eagle Springs and the unexplained death of a twelve-year-old boy. He'd tossed and turned most of the night, worrying that he'd wake Martha. The times when he could drift off to sleep, Buck Ramsey's face would float before his eyes, the steely gaze he gave to his surroundings, the cold stare that seemed to peer into Gabe's soul. When he wasn't thinking about Ramsey, his thoughts were on the circumstances surrounding Johnny's murder and the mysterious disappearance of his mother. No matter how often he examined the versions of the story told by Harvey and Widow Hawkins, the same things kept coming up missing. There was no apparent motive for killing the boy, and no explanation that made any sense for Anna Ramsey's sudden departure. He couldn't shake the feeling that both Harvey and Clara knew more than they were willing to tell. The more Gabe considered their stories, the more he doubted them. Today he planned to talk to Harvey again, to see if the old man would reveal anything else.

When the cow's udder was dry, he took the milk pail and carried it toward the house. The dog trotted eagerly beside him, hoping to lick up a few spills if the bucket was carried carelessly. Gabe climbed the back steps, then poured a small amount of milk into the dog's dish. "There you are, Red," he said. "Now you can quit your constant begging. Pretty soon you'll be too fat to catch a rabbit anyway. Might as well have been born with just three legs, fat as you're gettin'."

He went inside, to find Martha busy at the stove preparing his eggs and bacon. The shoat he'd butchered after the first frost made plenty of meat to see them through the winter. He put the milk beside the butter churn, then poured himself a cup of coffee.

"You tossed and turned all night," Martha said. "How come you couldn't sleep?"

"Thinkin' about Johnny Ramsey, I reckon. Trying to figure why anyone would want to kill him."

Martha gazed out the kitchen window a moment, the way she did when she was doing her deepest thinking. "Maybe he saw something he wasn't supposed to see," she wondered aloud. "Maybe someone wanted to silence him, so he couldn't talk about it."

Gabe took a seat at the table, blowing steam from the rim of his cup. "What could a twelve-year-old boy have seen around Eagle Springs that was worth killing him to keep him quiet?"

Martha was stumped. She shook her head. "I don't have that figured out. Hardly anything goes on around here that important, I don't suppose."

"I forgot to serve those papers on Clarence yesterday," Gabe muttered. "Got so busy with this Ramsey thing I plumb forgot to head out there. The mule's doin' better today, so I'll ride it to town and then out to Clarence's. I sure do hate the idea of servin' the papers. Always did like Clarence."

Martha brought him a plate of fried eggs and bacon. Yesterday's warmed-over biscuits sat on the table beside a jar of honey and a bowl of butter. Gabe found he had no appetite, thinking about delivering the tax notice to Clarence Cummings. He picked up a fork and started to eat disinterestedly.

Martha returned to the table with her own plate. "I remember Anna Ramsey was real pretty. She had long dark hair and real smooth skin. She wasn't here all that long, but I remember how all the menfolk used to stare at her when she walked to the store. She didn't hardly look old enough to have a boy in the army."

"Some women have kids real young," he offered, trying to imagine what Anna looked like. "Being she was a widow so early, she could have gotten married again, I reckon. I wonder why she didn't."

Martha's thoughtful expression returned. "Never knew of her having a suitor. Maybe I was too young to notice things like that. Seems like we had plenty of eligible bachelors back then, before so many got killed in the war. If she had any gentlemen callers, Alice will remember it."

Gabe found himself dreading the talk with Alice, after what Martha told her about going naked around the house. "She'll ask me if you wear clothes most of the time. I just know she's gonna ask me."

Martha wasn't paying any attention, staring blankly at the wall. "I wonder if that's the reason Anna disappeared. Maybe she ran off with a man who wanted to marry her, figuring she'd come back for Johnny. But then she heard he'd been killed after she left?"

"Hard to believe," Gabe replied. "Only

thing is, why didn't she tell somebody she was leavin'?"

"Maybe she did, only that person is keeping it quiet."

"But why?" he asked her, unable to guess a logical reason for someone's silence if Anna Ramsey left town to get married. "Besides, wouldn't she come back as soon as she heard about her son? She would have seen to making the final arrangements for having Johnny buried."

Martha shrugged and looked down at her plate. "None of it makes much sense to me."

Hiram Warner's small farm lay east of the river, just below the spot where Justin Creek joined the Leon. It wasn't much of a place, barely a hundred acres of bottomland. Gabe rode the mule toward the house, listening to the squeak of his old McClellan saddle, admiring the neatly tended fields belonging to Alice's husband, promising himself that one day he and Martha would quit sharecropping to own their own land.

"Hello the house!" he shouted as a spotted dog began to bark from the front porch, hair bristling on its neck. He hauled back on the mule's reins, waiting to be invited down.

The front door opened. Alice came out, wiping her hands on her apron. She shaded her eyes from the morning sun and, when she recognized Gabe, smiled and waved him to the house. "Hiram's gone to the gin," she said, watching Gabe dismount. "He said he wouldn't be long."

"I wanted to talk to you," he told her, leading the mule to the porch steps. "Martha sends her best. She told me to ask you about the time Johnny Ramsey got killed. She said you'd remember the boy, and his mother."

Alice's face darkened. "It has to do with Buck coming back yesterday, don't it?" she asked. "Word's all over town that he came back to find the man who shot his brother. Hope Huffman couldn't wait to tell me about it. She drove all the way out here in the buggy just to tell me Buck was here. I suppose you know he's been locked away in prison."

"I know," Gabe answered, certain he would have to listen to a litany of local gossip before he got what he came for. Alice Warner was widely regarded as the longest-winded woman in Coryell County. "Tell me what you remember about Johnny, about the day he died, and anything you remember about Anna."

Alice took a deep breath, building up wind, Gabe knew. She might have once been called pretty, before she started gaining weight. Gabe always suspected she ate a lot to keep up her strength for all the talking she did.

"Johnny was found dead early in April of '64," Alice began, settling on a porch step to tell her story, spreading her flour-sack skirt around her. "He'd been dead most of the night, according to Sheriff Barnes. He claimed he could tell by the dry blood around the body. Then somebody discovered that Johnny's mother was missing. All her clothes were gone from the house. They lived down by the creek, just past Clara Hawkins in that old tumble-down house. That's where they found Johnny — right beside the cow shed. Sheriff Barnes asked Clara if she heard the gun go off, but you know how deaf she is. She swore she didn't hear a gun, and she didn't see the wagon when Johnny's mother drove away. It was all real strange, the way it happened. Buck was fightin' the war, and when he didn't come back, folks figured he'd gotten himself killed someplace."

"Martha told me Anna was pretty," Gabe said. "She was a widow woman, kinda on the young side?"

Alice nodded. "She was beautiful. Longest black hair you ever saw, maybe thirty-two or three, back when it all happened. Plenty of men stared at her. She had a real pretty figure too. She was a widow by the time they moved to Eagle Springs. She never said what come of her husband, only that he was dead and

68

she had to raise two boys on her own."

"Did she ever have . . . any gentleman callers?" he asked.

For a moment, Alice seemed to be lost in thought. "Not the ordinary kind. Cleve Wade used to drop by now and then, to see if there was anything she needed. Bein' the richest man in the whole county, I suppose he felt sorry for her, with two kids to raise by herself."

"I don't reckon that's so unusual," Gabe said, thinking out loud. "Cleve raised a daughter. Martha told me his wife died givin' birth to Peggy Sue."

Alice agreed. "Folks who know him claim he's real generous with his neighbors. I think he was only bein' generous to Johnny's mother. Never knew of him to court Miz Ramsey outright. He never took her flowers or anything like that."

"How well did you know Johnny?" Gabe asked, when questions about Anna seemed to be a dead end.

"Not hardly at all," Alice replied, like she didn't need time to think. "He was a real quiet boy. Shy, I'd call him. He hardly ever said a word at school, except when Miss Tarver asked him a question. I remember he was always daydreamin', staring out a window like his mind was someplace else. I was a year

69

older, so we didn't talk much. Besides, I hardly ever remember him talking to girls. I suppose Bobby Cummings was his best friend. They went swimming down at the creek sometimes."

"Can you think of why anybody'd want to kill him?" Gabe asked.

Alice shook her head. "Nobody else could, either. It's the biggest mystery ever to happen in this town. Only people tended to forget about it when word started coming about how many men from this part of the county lost their lives to the war. Down at the church, Preacher Sims used to read the list of names most every Sunday. Folks were cryin' all day, seemed like. Pretty soon, everybody forgot about Johnny Ramsey and his mother. There were plenty of tears to be shed, more than enough to go round."

Gabe looked up at the sky. "I'll ask Bobby Cummings if he remembers anything about Johnny. I've got to go out there later on to serve some papers."

Alice suddenly fixed him with a look, and he quickly realized his mistake. Alice would tell everyone within shouting distance that the Cummings family was being served with a tax levy.

"They haven't been able to pay their taxes," she said. It wasn't a question.

"Official business," Gabe replied, avoiding her eyes. "Much obliged for the information about the Ramseys. I'm looking into it."

"You be careful around that Buck," she warned as Gabe was mounting the mule. "I wouldn't want to hear how dear sweet Martha got to be a widow so soon after she took her wedding vows. Why, the two of you haven't even had your first child."

"I can take care of myself around Buck Ramsey," he promised, pulling the mule away from the porch.

Alice stood up and smiled. "Aren't you the confident one now, Sheriff Miller? That badge on your chest made you grow up in a hurry. Remember to give my best to Martha. Tell her it's high time she got on with having some children, like a wife's supposed to. She told me you were the bashful type . . . that you were shy. A shy husband won't father many children, Gabriel Miller!"

He knew his face was turning red before he could get the mule swung around to ride back down the lane. "I'll give her your regards," he said quickly. He'd known all along that Alice would make some remark like that. "Tell Hiram I was by," he added over his shoulder, drumming his heels into the mule's ribs to make an escape before Alice said any more about things that shouldn't be talked about in public.

He was grateful when the mule struck a trot, despite its sorefooted condition from the founder. He wouldn't look back to wave at Alice, nor did he intend to mention to Martha what Alice said about having children. At the proper time, he meant to tell his wife that such matters should remain a secret. If he wanted Alice Warner to know what went on inside the Miller house, not to mention having that same information spread over half the county, he would post a notice in the Gatesville newspaper. Which was about as likely as having snow in July across the middle of Texas.

On the road back to Eagle Springs, he thought about the things Alice told him. Anna Ramsey was more than pretty — Alice had called her beautiful. Then there was the mention of visits by Cleveland Wade, another surprise. Cleve Wade was a rough-cut sort, brash, boastful about his wealth. Some folks liked him, although Gabe suspected it was due to his power and influence in county politics. Cleve hadn't been willing to support Gabe in the election last fall, and Gabe had won the sheriff's job by the narrowest of margins. Cleve had thrown his support behind his own candidate, a bachelor cowboy named Will Jameson, who did day work for area ranches. Few people had a very high opinion of Jameson, due to his regular habit of getting drunk every Saturday night at the Broken Spoke. Winning the election hadn't actually put Gabe at odds with Cleve Wade, but neither could it be said relations were all that friendly between them. Cleve had wanted his own hand-picked man in the sheriff's office so he could own the badge in almost the same way he owned the best land in this end of the county.

Gabe wondered where Buck Ramsey might be this morning. As he'd ridden by the tent where Ramsey made camp the day before, he found it empty. No doubt, Ramsey was off prowling the countryside, seeking the same answers as Gabe was.

One thing was certain . . . now that a hardened gunman was on the loose around Eagle Springs, poking into affairs most folks had all but forgotten, things wouldn't be the same for quite a spell. Not until Buck Ramsey found what he was looking for and then rode elsewhere, if the killer's identity could be found at this late date. Gabe only hoped Ramsey's search wouldn't leave a mound of fresh earth beyond the hill at the cemetery.

CHAPTER 7

The Cummings farm was about six miles northwest of town, one of the poorest plots of land in that end of Coryell County, lying just below the rocky dry wash known as Beaver Draw. Gabe remembered it was the place where Harvey lost the tracks of Anna Ramsey's wagon. It was easy to see why tracks were hard to follow there. Solid slabs of limestone stretched as far as the eye could see in every direction. Gabe slowed the mule when he came to the bottom of the draw.

"She knew nobody could trail her across these rocks," he muttered to himself, frowning down at the ground. "She meant to make sure nobody followed her, if she was the one drivin' the wagon that night. It would take somebody who knew this part of the country to know about the rocks. Miz Ramsey hadn't lived here all that long, so maybe she didn't know about it? Maybe somebody else was drivin' her wagon?"

The mule's ears flipped back and forth at

the sound of his voice, reminding him how foolish he would seem if someone saw him out here talking to himself. Looking up and down the length of the draw, Gabe was more certain than ever that whoever was driving the wagon knew the lay of the land. It was unlikely that a woman would come out here for any reason, unless she was paying a call on the Cummings family. Then he remembered Alice said that Bobby Cummings could be called Johnny Ramsey's closest friend, so that might explain why Anna knew to bring the wagon this way when she left town. Thus, Gabe figured he could probably discard the idea that someone else was driving the wagon, if Anna had ever driven out to the Cummings place before. "I'll ask," he told himself, urging the mule forward again.

West of the draw, he came in sight of the Cummings farm, a ramshackle old house that befit the family's poor circumstances. A hay barn and a low-roofed hog shed sat behind the house in a similar state of disrepair. The hour was approaching noon when Gabe rode up, and he could smell something cooking as the wind carried smoke from the kitchen stovepipe. He hailed the house between cupped hands and waited to dismount. Moments later, a sagging plank door opened inward, then Clarence came out, dressed in mended overalls faded by too many washings. When Clarence recognized Gabe, he nodded meekly and waved him down. By the look on Clarence's face, he had no doubts why Gabe had come.

"Howdy, Gabe," he said. "I reckon I know why you're here. We ain't got the cash money to pay them taxes. Hardly rained at all out here last summer. Barely made a crop with the corn. Can't sell none of the cotton I raised, either. Got six bales over at the gin, but it won't fetch a price. It figures you come to serve my papers."

"I'm real sorry to have to do it, Clarence," he said, removing the levy notice from an inside pocket of his coat. "Judge Green ordered me to bring it out and I ain't got much of a choice. Hope you believe me about that. I'm a farmer myself, so I know what a dry year can do." Stepping to the ground, he carried the folded paper to the porch and handed it to Clarence.

"How long have I got before they hold the tax sale?" he asked, taking the notice in calloused hands without opening it. "Can't read, so you'll have to tell me what it says. Bobby, he can read a little, only he ain't here no more. Found a job over at the gin in Waco. Said he was tired of bein' poor."

One look at the farm was proof enough that

the Cummings family was dirt poor. "The notice gives you sixty days before the county sheriff holds the sale. Maybe we can all sell our cotton for a decent price by then."

Clarence wagged his head doubtfully. "Ain't likely. Roy Culpepper told me when I was down at the store to buy some buttons that cotton prices were liable to stay down for a year or two. By then we won't have no place to live. I've got six mouths to feed, an' Bonnie's swelled up with another baby."

"I know times have been hard," Gabe agreed. Nothing he could say to Clarence would change things. "I was hoping to get a chance to talk to Bobby. Alice Warner told me that Bobby used to be friends with Johnny Ramsey."

Clarence scowled. "Seems I oughta know that name," he said.

"He was the boy who got shot down by the creek a few years back," Gabe told him.

Sudden recognition changed the expression on the farmer's face. He looked askance, making Gabe wonder why.

"Now I remember," Clarence said quietly. "Him'n Bobby used to swim some. Bobby got real torn up about it when the boy was killed."

Gabe formed his next question carefully. "Did Johnny and his ma ever come out here for a visit in their wagon?"

Clarence shook his head. "Never did. I could nearly swear to it."

Gabe looked over his shoulder, in the direction of Beaver Draw. "Sheriff Barnes trailed their wagon to the bottom of the draw yonder, the day after Johnny got shot. He told me he lost the tracks in all that rock. Nobody ever saw Miz Ramsey again after that. She just up and disappeared."

"Seems I remember that too," Clarence replied, looking at something on the distant horizon.

"I was wondering," Gabe continued, "if maybe you saw or heard a wagon pass by that night. If Miz Ramsey kept going the same direction, she'd have to pass right by your place."

Clarence shook his head — it might have been too quickly, in Gabe's estimation. Or was he once again letting his imagination run wild?

"Never saw or heard no wagon that I recall. That's a long time back to remember."

"I'm looking into it," Gabe explained.

"How come?" Clarence asked, sounding downright bewildered.

"The boy's brother finally made it back to Eagle Springs. He wants to know how it happened, maybe find out who killed him. Buck Ramsey was away in prison until just lately. Now he wants to get to the bottom of it, if he can."

Clarence swallowed, making his Adam's apple bob up and down inside his skinny neck. "What did Harvey tell him? I'm sure he asked Harvey about it . . ."

This time, Gabe was sure Clarence was afraid of something. "Harvey didn't have much to say, only that they found the boy early that morning, and that Miz Ramsey had come up missing. I get the feeling there's more to the story. Maybe you can tell me if there's anything else I oughta know."

Clarence scuffed a badly worn lace-up shoe on a porch board, looking down now. "I wouldn't know nothin' about it," he said. "We never did live in town. Always lived right here."

Gabe was convinced Clarence was hiding something. "I figured you must have heard that wagon pass by. A wagon makes a lot of noise crossing rocky ground."

"Nope," Clarence said flatly, still watching his shoe. "I never heard no wagon. I'd remember it."

When it was clear Clarence wouldn't say anything else, Gabe turned to mount the mule. "Time I headed back to town," he said, pulling himself over the saddle. "Sorry about having to bring that notice out. I'll ask a favor of you. If you happen to remember seeing that wagon pass by the night Johnny was killed, or if maybe your wife remembers, I'd be grateful if you sent me word. I've got a feeling Buck Ramsey's gonna stay around Eagle Springs until he gets some answers, or finds out there aren't any to be had, so long after it happened. Ramsey's a gunman, a real dangerous man to have hanging around town. It's my job to keep law and order in this neck of the woods, and I'd sure hate to have somebody get killed in my jurisdiction over something that happened ten years ago. I'd be obliged for anything you or your wife can remember, if that wagon happened to come this way. Soon as I know what happened to Miz Ramsey, I'll be closer to finding out who shot her son."

"I'll ask Bonnie," Clarence muttered, as though his mind were on something else. "I'll be tryin' to raise that tax money. Can't sell my sows or we can't raise any hogs. My corn goes to feed the hogs, so I can't sell it neither. These have sure been some mighty hard times."

"I can see you're in a predicament," Gabe said, pulling the mule away from the porch. "Sorry I had to be the one to make things seem worse. I'm only doing my job, Clarence."

Clarence shook his head, like he understood, glancing down to the paper in his hand just as Gabe was riding off. Serving the levy on such a desperately poor family was making Gabe feel sick to his stomach.

He rode to Beaver Draw and looked back at the house, surer than ever that Clarence and his wife would have heard a noisy wagon rattling over the rocks. "He saw or heard that wagon," Gabe assured himself, "only I can't figure why he won't talk. Maybe he saw someone else in that wagon seat, somebody he knew, someone he's trying to protect, someone from around here, maybe."

Coming away from the Cummings farm with more questions than answers, he was staring into space and almost missed seeing the distant outline of a rider farther to the north. When his eyes focused, he recognized the man and the horse. "What the heck is Buck Ramsey doing way out here?"

He turned the mule and heeled it to a slow trot, being careful to keep the animal's sore hooves off the worst of the sharp stones. Ramsey saw him and halted his roan on the crest of a rocky hill, waiting for Gabe to arrive.

Ramsey nodded slightly when Gabe pulled back on the mule, allowing Gabe to speak first.

"I wondered why you're out here," Gabe explained when Ramsey said nothing.

Ramsey pointed to the draw where Gabe had ridden. "That's where the old sheriff said he lost the wagon tracks. I wanted to see the place for myself," he said, talking so softly Gabe had to strain to hear every word.

Gabe looked over his shoulder. "That's Beaver Draw, all right. There's a farmhouse on the other side . . . you can't see it from here. It belongs to Clarence Cummings. I just asked Clarence if he remembered seeing your ma's wagon pass by that morning. He claims he didn't see or hear a thing, only I had the feeling he wasn't telling me the whole truth."

Ramsey's expression did not change. "Neither is the old woman, and I'm not buyin' the sheriff's story just yet. Maybe all they need is a push."

Gabe didn't like the sound of what Ramsey said. "If there's any pushing to be done, I'll be the one to do it. I'm the one wearing the badge."

The gunman's gaze came to rest on Gabe's face. For a time, he said nothing, working the muscles in his cheeks. "Then start doin' your job the way it oughta be done, Sheriff. Don't try my patience by wasting more time. You've talked to three people, and I know two of them are lying."

Gabe met Ramsey's stare with a look of his own. "I know how to do my job," he said with a confidence he didn't really feel just then. "I aim to talk to Miz Hawkins again.

Harvey too, if he's feeling better."

For the moment, Ramsey seemed satisfied. "Maybe I'll talk to this Clarence Cummings myself," he said quietly, studying Beaver Draw again. "No law against that, is there?"

"Just so all you do is talk," Gabe replied, taking a deep breath. "I feel sorry for Clarence and his family. They're poor as church mice. I just served him with papers that'll take away his farm for back taxes if he can't raise the money."

Ramsey glared at Gabe. Suddenly there was a smoldering fire behind his pale eyes. "That's because we've got a goddamn carpetbagger government now," he spat. "A bunch of Yankee politicians run this state and the rest of the South. The bastards won't be satisfied until they own everything."

The heat in Ramsey's voice made Gabe think twice about offering any argument, that acting as sheriff wasn't quite the same thing. "I only serve the papers they send over. I said I felt sorry for the Cummingses."

Ramsey grunted and lifted his reins. The roan started off the hill, ending the conversation. Gabe watched the lanky gunman ride toward the wagon ruts leading to the bottom of the draw, sensing that Ramsey was only a heartbeat away from stirring up real trouble around Eagle Springs. He'd never met a man quite like Buck Ramsey: It was like sitting in a room with a powderkeg, watching a lighted fuse burn down to the end. Gabe felt he was helpless to stop events from unfolding in the coming days as Ramsey went about his own investigation of his brother's death and the disappearance of his mother. The same queasy feeling in the pit of his stomach after leaving the Cummings farm had now grown worse.

Gabe was sure he could predict things were coming to a head as he urged the mule back toward town. It was like sighting a bank of storm clouds on the horizon. A storm was brewing, and when it struck Eagle Springs, all hell would break loose.

CHAPTER 8

Harvey's wife showed him to the bedroom. For a moment, it appeared Harvey was asleep, until his eyelids fluttered, then his eyes opened and he focused on Gabe.

"How're you feeling?" Gabe asked, noticing more fresh blood on the towel beside Harvey's pillow.

"Maybe not so good today," Harvey replied, sounding weaker than the day before.

"I'll only stay a minute," Gabe promised. "I rode out to Beaver Draw today — had to serve papers on Clarence Cummings. That draw is where you lost the tracks from Anna Ramsey's wagon. It's easy to see why, all that rock. Made me wonder why Miz Ramsey would head in that direction. It's like she knew nobody could follow her away from the draw. Trouble is, I can't quite figure out how she knew about the place. I asked Clarence if she'd ever been out there. He said he couldn't remember seeing her. Clarence acted mighty strange when I started asking him about

85

Johnny's death. He swore he never heard Miz Ramsey's wagon that night, or the next morning. That part don't figure either. A wagon would make a lot of noise on rocky ground."

Harvey scowled a little. "What do you mean, Clarence acted strange?"

"Nervous, I reckon you'd call it. Like he knew more'n he was willing to say."

The ensuing silence was much too long, in Gabe's estimation, and Harvey's eyes drifted over to his bedroom window, so he wasn't looking at Gabe when he spoke.

"Where's Buck?" Harvey asked, as though he didn't want to talk about Clarence.

"He pitched a camp down by the creek yesterday. Just now, he was out at Beaver Draw himself, having a look around. He aims to stay until he's satisfied, one way or the other."

Harvey nodded, still watching the window. "He's liable to stir up a hornet's nest. He's nothin' but trouble."

"He wants to know who killed his brother and find out where his ma went. I don't think he'll leave until he gets some answers."

"I suppose you're right," Harvey agreed, sighing. "Did he talk to Clara about it?"

"We both did. She acted funny about it, too, if you want my opinion, like there might have been something she's trying to hide."

Harvey looked at him then. "Can't imagine

what it would be," he said. "She told me she didn't see or hear a thing that night. I investigated it the best I could, only I kept coming up with the same dead ends. I always sort of suspicioned that maybe some drifter came along — tried to rob Anna in the dark. The boy tried to stop the robbery with that old shotgun and got himself killed. Then that drifter could have forced Anna to drive her wagon someplace, which makes sense if he was afoot when he hit town. Me, I've always held to the drifter theory. It's about the only way to explain what happened."

Gabe saw several things wrong with Harvey's idea. "Why would a drifter rob one of the poorest families in town? That house ain't nothin' but a shack. And if it was a robber who shot Johnny, then why did he allow Miz Ramsey time to pack up her clothes? If he'd just killed somebody, looks like he'd have been in a hurry to clear out, worrying that folks heard the gunshot."

Harvey started to cough. His chest heaved mightily, then he spit a mouthful of blood into the towel. More spasms followed the first, bringing Bernice into the room.

"You'd better go, Gabriel," she said, hurrying to Harvey's bedside. "He needs his rest."

"Sure thing," Gabe told her, backing for

the door. "I hope he gets to feeling better soon." He let himself out the front door while listening to Harvey cough, thinking how much worse the old man looked today. "I doubt he'll live much longer," Gabe whispered, climbing aboard the mule for the ride home to have lunch with Martha.

He rode through Eagle Springs, considering how little he'd learned from Harvey just now. The notion that some drifter had come along to rob the Ramseys didn't make any sense and Gabe wondered if it could have been an attempt to steer him in the wrong direction. He was still nagged by the feeling that Harvey was keeping something from him.

"Alice was chock-full of information," he told Martha, over a plate piled high with boiled turnip greens and ham hock.

"I told you she'd know," Martha said, taking a modest portion of greens. "Did she tell you anything that might help you solve it?"

He shook his head. "Not really, only that Anna Ramsey was very beautiful. Bobby Cummings was Johnny's best friend, just about the only friend he had. I wanted to talk to Bobby when I rode out to serve Clarence his papers, only I found out Bobby took a job over at Waco. Clarence acted sorta strange when I asked him what he remembered about the shooting. Beaver Draw is where Harvey lost Anna's wagon tracks, so I asked Clarence if he recalled hearing a wagon pass by that night. Right off, maybe too quick, he said he didn't remember a wagon. It don't appear I learned anything today that puts me any closer to solving it."

Martha was nibbling on a forkful of greens when she said, "Maybe it won't ever be solved, because it can't be. Harvey did his best and couldn't find out anything."

Gabe paused with a mouthful of food, wondering if Harvey had really done his best. He swallowed and said, "I'm not all that sure Harvey has told me all he knows. Same goes for Miz Hawkins and Clarence. Trouble is, I can't begin to guess what they could be hiding."

Martha watched him silently for a moment. "It makes me wonder if all three of them knew someone who was involved. It's about the only reason they'd keep quiet, to protect somebody they all knew. Somebody they liked."

Gabe nodded thoughtfully. "Or somebody they were all afraid of. But who the heck could that be? Nearly everybody gets along reasonable well in this end of the county."

"I say they're trying to protect someone, if they aren't telling you the whole truth about what happened," she argued.

"It's one heck of a puzzle," he said. "Worst

is, I've got Buck Ramsey looking over my shoulder. Just this morning, he was out near Beaver Draw, poking around. He claims to know Clara Hawkins and Harvey are both lying about something. He says they need to be pushed to tell the truth."

Martha looked up quickly from her food. "What did he mean by that?"

Gabe took a deep breath. "I suppose it means that he intends to start asking questions with a gun in his hand."

He was building a fire in the potbelly stove at the office toward the middle of the afternoon when he heard a horse outside. Glancing through the window, he saw a big sorrel stallion come to a halt in front of the door. Peggy Sue Wade jumped from an expensive hand-tooled saddle, decorated with silver conchos, and tied the stud at the hitchrail. She was dressed in a fleece-lined sheepskin coat and denims, her dark red hair done in a single braid that almost reached her waist. She looked through the window and smiled at Gabe, then climbed to the boardwalk and came inside, allowing a gust of cold wind into the building before she closed the door.

"Hello, Gabriel," she said, smiling again, revealing rows of even, sparkling teeth. "I've got something for you from my pa. I'm glad

I found you in town."

He closed the door to the potbelly and dusted off his hands. "Good to see you again, Peggy Sue," he said, grinning, trying not to grin too broadly when he noticed how tightly her denims fit. "What did your pa send?"

She took an envelope from a jacket pocket and handed it to Gabe. Inside was a bundle of bank notes. He puzzled over the money briefly, knowing Peggy Sue would explain. A folded paper was with the money and before the girl said anything, he recognized the tax levy he had just delivered to Clarence Cummings.

"It's the back taxes for the Cummings family," Peggy Sue began, watching Gabe's face. "Pa said he was loaning Clarence the money, on account of they're so poor and they're our neighbors. Clarence came over right after you served him. He talked to my pa for a long time. You could see he was upset."

"Didn't mean to upset him any more than necessary," Gabe told her, frowning at the contents of the envelope. "I was only doing my job. It couldn't be helped."

"I understand," the girl replied in a gentle voice. "Everybody knows those papers aren't your fault. Taxes have to be paid, even when times are hard the way they are now."

"Your pa's being mighty generous," Gabe

observed, idly thumbing through the currency.

"He can be real nice when he wants to be, when he likes somebody," she said. "If you got to know him, you'd like him, too. It was nothing personal when he supported Will Jameson to be the sheriff. Will works for us from time to time, and Pa said he hardly knew you at all."

"It's okay," he answered, thinking how truly generous Cleve Wade was to lend Clarence almost a hundred dollars, three years' worth of taxes on Clarence's land, which was the same length as the drought across most of Coryell County. "I never held it against your pa that he voted for Will. Honest, I didn't."

The girl's face grew serious. "My pa's worried for Clarence now. There's this outlaw who just got out of prison that came to talk to Clarence today. His name is Buck Ramsey, and Pa said he threatened Clarence with a gun. Ramsey's brother was killed here in Eagle Springs a long time ago."

"I've met Buck Ramsey," Gabe said, made wary by the news that Ramsey threatened Clarence Cummings with a gun. "Are you sure Ramsey pulled a gun on Clarence?"

"That's what Pa told me. Pa and Clarence talked for a long time, back in Pa's study.

Right after Clarence left, Pa sent me to town with this money. He told me he was feeling real sorry for the family. And he said to tell you that Buck Ramsey drew his gun on Clarence. You could tell Clarence was real scared."

"Tell your pa I'll look into it," Gabe said. "I won't allow Ramsey to threaten anyone with a gun. And tell your pa I'll get this money over to Judge Green right away. He'll cancel the levy and that will be the end of it."

Peggy Sue made a half turn for the door. She smiled at Gabe, reminding him of how pretty she was.

"I'll tell Pa what you said. I know he'll be grateful if you can stop that outlaw from bothering Clarence. Like I told you before, they're our neighbors." She waved and walked out of the office, leaving Gabe with a knot forming in his belly, wondering if Buck Ramsey had just begun to show everyone around Eagle Springs just how deadly serious he was about finding out what happened to his family.

Gabe tucked the envelope into a coat pocket as Peggy Sue mounted her horse. For the time being, one unpleasant task was out of the way. There would be no tax sale at the Cummings farm two months from now, and that would be a blessing. Cleveland Wade's generosity was a complete surprise. Lending Clarence the tax money was the act of a good friend. Gabe wondered if he could have misjudged Cleve all this time. Perhaps, underneath his gruff exterior, he was a better man than Gabe had thought him to be.

The girl rode off, leaving Gabe alone with his dilemma. He knew he would have to confront Ramsey about the gun he pulled on Clarence Cummings. No matter how tough the gunfighter's reputation made him sound, Gabe couldn't allow him to ask questions at gunpoint all over the county.

He walked over to the desk and took the gun and holster from a bottom drawer. The gun, along with a shotgun and a Winchester rifle, came with the job. In his heart, Gabe knew he wasn't any great shakes with a pistol, and perhaps only a respectable shot with a rifle. Facing Ramsey with a sidearm, he wouldn't have much of a chance.

He strapped on the gun belt and checked the loads in the Colt .44, wondering if wearing a gun when he confronted Ramsey could be a mistake. Ramsey might feel the gun made them equal, thus he'd have no twinges of conscience when he shot Gabe.

At that, Gabe chuckled to himself. Gunmen like Buck Ramsey weren't burdened with a conscience.

CHAPTER 9

He took the hobbles off the mule as dusk was settling over the Leon valley, meaning to ride by Ramsey's camp on his way home. For most of the afternoon he'd been dreading the meeting with Ramsey, carefully choosing what he would say about the affair out at the Cummings farm. He wondered if Ramsey would bristle when he made the accusation. Or would he maintain the same calm he always seemed to have? Just once, the gunman had revealed some powerful emotion when he talked about what Reconstruction was doing to the South. His anger disappeared quickly enough right after that, but it had given Gabe a glimpse of what Ramsey would be like when he was on the prod.

He cinched the saddle and mounted for the ride down to the creek, being careful to cover the gun with his coat as soon as he rode away from the office. Farther down Main Street, lights burned behind windows at the saloon. The mercantile and the general store had already closed. With the approach of nightfall the wind died down while the temperature dropped. Gabe could see frosty breath rolling from the mule's muzzle as it carried him toward Clara Hawkins's house, and the creekbank just beyond.

When he drew near Ramsey's tent, he could see there was no fire, and Ramsey's horse was gone. "Off someplace, nosing around," Gabe muttered, heeling the mule for home. As he rode behind Clara's house, he paid close attention to the distance between her place and the abandoned Ramsey home. It struck him again just how close the dwellings were. "Even if Miz Hawkins was deaf as a post back then, I just know she must have heard that gunshot," he mumbled to himself.

Martha was waiting supper when he walked in the house. She turned from the stove as he hung up his coat and hat. Right off, she noticed the gun belt around his waist.

"Why are you wearing a gun?" she asked, her face dark with concern.

He began unbuckling the belt as he replied, "Just to be on the safe side," not wanting to worry her.

"It's because of Buck Ramsey, isn't it."

He wouldn't tell her an outright lie. "Peggy Sue Wade claimed that Ramsey stuck a gun in Clarence Cummings's face this afternoon. I can't allow Ramsey to do that. I'd planned to talk to him, only he wasn't down at the creek when I rode by on my way home."

"Why would anybody pull a gun on Clarence Cummings?" she asked, furrowing her brow.

He took a seat at the table after the gun belt was hanging on a peg. "I reckon Ramsey thinks Clarence saw Anna drive by in the wagon when she left this county. I asked Clarence if he remembered a wagon. He claims he never saw a wagon. Ramsey must figure he's lying."

Martha brought him a plate of leftover greens, her expression still serious. "I wish you wouldn't wear that pistol," she said softly, as though she said it to herself. "I'll worry myself sick about it."

He smiled, to reassure her. "Don't fret over it. I just don't want Buck Ramsey to think I'll back down when I tell him to leave his gun holstered."

"Oh, Gabe," she whispered, coming around the table, wiping her hands on the front of her apron. She stood behind him and put her arms around his neck. "Please don't wear that gun. There has to be another way to stop what Ramsey is doing."

"I told you not to worry," he scolded, patting her hand gently. "I can take care of myself."

She bent over to kiss his cheek. "I know you can," she said, "but I'll still worry until that outlaw leaves. I hope it's soon. By the way, you mentioned that Peggy Sue told you about what Ramsey did to Clarence. Did you happen to see her in town?"

"Her pa sent her. When Cleve Wade learned about the tax papers I served on Clarence, he made Clarence a loan to pay the taxes. I've got the money in my coat. First thing tomorrow, I'll take it over to Judge Green. It sure surprised me, that Cleve would do something like that just because him and Clarence are neighbors. I never had a high opinion of Cleve. Maybe I've been wrong about him all along."

Martha went to the stove for her supper. "I've heard some say he's a generous man to those he likes. He acts real brash most of the time, like his money makes him better'n most folks. Can't argue that he's not bein' good to the Cummingses, though." She came to the table and sat down. "Did you find out anything more today?" she asked.

"I talked to Harvey again. He didn't shed any new light on things. I know he's real sick, but he gives the impression he don't want to talk about what happened to Johnny. He acts like he wants me to believe some drifter came through town that day, trying to rob the Ramseys. That's how he explains Anna's disappearance, that a drifter made Miz Ramsey haul him someplace in her wagon."

"She would have come back to bury her boy, if she was able," Martha insisted.

He nodded thoughtfully. "Besides that, why would anybody rob such a poor family? Harvey's idea don't make any sense."

He'd ridden to town early, to get a good start on the trip to Gatesville with the tax money. He unlocked the office a half hour past daybreak, allowing time to question Ramsey about the incident out at the Cummings farm. He could see a curl of smoke coming from Ramsey's camp and started to feel edgy again. Crossing over to the desk, he opened a drawer for the reports he needed to take to the judge, outlining his official actions for the past few weeks, a job requirement he neither disliked nor liked. He wasn't much good at paperwork; spelling sometimes gave him trouble. He struck a match to the lantern and glanced through the reports briefly, until he was satisfied everything was in order, hoping important words were spelled right. As he extinguished the lantern a few minutes later, he heard running footsteps in the early-morning silence. Someone was hurrying toward the office and it puzzled him.

When he walked outside to look northwest, he saw a slender girl running in his direction, her loose-fitting dress flapping about her. She wore no coat despite the December weather. For a time, he did not recognize her.

"Sheriff Miller!" the girl cried, when she was still a hundred yards away. "Come quick! Somebody shot my pa!"

He waited for her at the end of the boardwalk, unable to guess her identity. She arrived badly out of breath, as though she'd run a tremendous distance to get there.

"Tell me what happened . . . tell me who got shot," he said, noticing the girl's worn-out shoes and tattered dress, guessing her age to be fourteen or so. "I don't know who you are . . ."

She clasped her ribs, as if her chest might explode, panting when she tried to talk. "I'm Nellie Cummings," she gasped. "We heard a gun go off down at the barn. Somebody shot my pa an' he's bleedin' real bad. Please come quick!"

The girl was Clarence's daughter. "You ran all the way to town?" he asked, wheeling around to close the office door.

She nodded, sobbing softly now. "Ma said there wasn't time to hitch up the mules. She's seein' to my pa, tryin' to stop him from bleedin'. She told my sister Sara to fetch up the team so they could drive Pa over to the doctor at Gatesville. She sent me to fetch you . . . I couldn't hardly run for all my cryin'."

Gabe boarded his mule quickly and offered the girl his hand to help her up behind the saddle. He glanced across town, to the smoke coming from Ramsey's camp fire, wondering if Ramsey had been the one who shot Clarence. Just now, after hearing what happened yesterday between them, Ramsey was the most likely suspect. "Climb up!" he shouted, when the girl simply stood there.

Nellie swung up behind him as he was drumming his heels into the mule's ribs. She put her arms around his waist and buried her face in the back of his coat. The mule struck a trot, then a slow lope away from the edge of town. Gabe could feel the girl shivering against him.

Just once, on a hilltop northwest of the office, he looked over his shoulder. From such a distance he couldn't be sure he saw Ramsey's horse near the gunman's tent. Down in his gut, he knew it had been Ramsey who shot Clarence early this morning. Gabe didn't need to see Ramsey's blue roan horse to know he'd ridden out there to force Clarence to tell him everything he knew about his mother's disappearance.

The six-mile ride to Beaver Draw aboard a mule was slower than Gabe wished it could be. Nellie cried most of the way. As soon as they rode out of the draw and were in sight of the house, she burst into more tears and sobbed, "Hurry! Hurry!"

On the way out, Gabe kept reminding himself that a serious wound would probably kill Clarence before he could reach the county's only doctor over in Gatesville. From the girl's description of the blood flow, it seemed unlikely that Clarence could survive a twenty-mile drive. When Gabe looked behind the house, he saw a team of brown mules tethered to a wheel of the family's ancient cotton wagon. No one was attempting to harness the mules now and Gabe was sure he knew what that meant.

They rode up to the barn. Nellie was off the mule's rump before Gabe could bring the animal to a halt. Hearing hoofbeats, Bonnie Cummings came to the door of the hay barn, her swollen stomach straining inside a dress sewn from flour sacking. Gabe saw blood all over the front of her dress as he jumped to the ground. He heard Bonnie crying as he hurried to the barn door.

"It's too late," Bonnie moaned, wiping tears from her eyes with the back of her hand, her body shaking with silent sobs now. "Clarence is dead. He died before we could get the team hitched to the wagon . . ."

He stopped in front of the woman, glancing past her to see inside the barn. "I'm sorry, Miz Cummings," he said. "We got here as quick as we could."

She nodded. "My poor Clarence," she said, hoarse from crying. "Just when things looked a little better on account of bein' able to pay them taxes . . ."

"I'll take a look at him," Gabe told her quietly. "Did you see who fired the shot?"

Bonnie wagged her head, absently fingering stray locks of graying brown hair behind her ear. "No," she whimpered. "I was makin' Clarence his breakfast. I heard this loud noise come from the shed. Clarence was sloppin' the hogs. I screamed for Nellie to git out of bed. We ran down with the lantern, seein' as it was still dark. That's when . . . we found him, lyin' over yonder in the straw." She started to cry openly again.

Gabe patted her shoulder, then he turned and walked past her into the barn. Right away, he saw a body near a mound of last summer's hay. He could smell the coppery scent of blood before he was halfway across the barn.

Clarence was lying on his back, sightless eyes aimed up at the rafters. A hole in the front of his bib overalls was covered with drying blood. Gabe knelt beside the body, frowning, trying to imagine why anyone would kill a harmless farmer like Clarence Cummings. "This makes Buck Ramsey a coward," he whispered to himself. "He shot an unarmed man. You're headed back to prison for this, Mr. Ramsey. Maybe to a hangman's gallows instead. It's what you rightly deserve, if you're the one who shot Clarence." Looking at the bullet hole, then at the dead man's face, he felt slightly nauseous. This was the first death he had ever seen where a gun had been the cause, making him question the wisdom of wearing one himself. Was this a glimpse of his own fate at the hands of the same cold-blooded killer who murdered Clarence?

"I won't run from him," he promised quietly.

He heard footsteps coming through the straw behind him. When he glanced over his shoulder, he saw Nellie approaching her father's body with tears streaming down her face. Gathered around the barn door, Bonnie stood with four more of her children, looking into the half dark where Clarence lay.

Gabe stood up. He spoke to Nellie. "No need to come any closer. It ain't a very pretty sight."

She stopped, then buried her face in her hands and wept. He walked over to her and took her arm gently.

"Let's go outside, Nellie. There's nothing more anyone can do in here."

They walked out in bright sunlight. Gabe aimed a thumb at the back of the barn. "I'll have a look around," he said to Bonnie. "Maybe I can find some tracks."

"I can tell you who done it, Sheriff," Bonnie said, anger creeping into her voice despite the tears. "He called himself Buck Ramsey, an' he claimed to be Johnny Ramsey's older brother. He was here yesterday, askin' questions. Clarence acted real scared after he rode off. That's when he took one of the mules over to the Wade ranch. Said he needed to talk to Cleveland Wade 'bout somethin' real important. I reckon it was the tax money he loaned us that they talked about."

"I'd already guessed this was Ramsey's doing," Gabe said, thinking ahead to the moment he would arrest Ramsey for Clarence's murder. He knew Ramsey wouldn't come quietly to the Gatesville jail. He wouldn't give up his gun peacefully — Gabe was sure of it. What he needed was enough evidence to convince Judge Green that Ramsey was the killer. The way things stood now, there weren't any witnesses. Was it enough that Ramsey had threatened Clarence with a gun the day before?

He trudged over to a corner of the barn and went carefully down the side, studying the ground for footprints. There had been so little rain in this part of the county that the soil was like iron. But Gabe knew the killer was likely to have left some trace of his presence behind. If he looked hard enough, Gabe was sure he could find something that would help pin the murder on Buck Ramsey.

Behind the barn was a stand of live oaks. "That's where he would have hidden his horse," Gabe thought aloud, starting for the grove. He didn't have to go far among the trees before he found something. At the base of a tree, he discovered fresh horse droppings.

Crouching down, he began a careful search for hoofprints, reading each stretch of thin topsoil, examining open spots where limestone lay bare. He found faint scratches here and there, but no complete prints that might identify the horse shoes. The ground, where there wasn't any rock, was simply too hard to reveal anything.

He straightened up a half hour later, gazing at the surrounding hills and untended fields where Clarence had raised his meager corn and cotton crops. A careful man would have avoided riding through tilled earth where hoofprints would be plain, but Gabe knew he must look anyway. Unlike the investigation ten years ago when Harvey searched for the identity of Johnny's killer, Gabe meant to leave no stone unturned in the death of Clarence Cummings. It simply wasn't enough to be certain that Buck Ramsey was responsible. Gabe needed evidence, and he meant to find it if the killer had left behind any telltale trace of his comings and goings.

CHAPTER 10

There were no hoofprints across any of the fields. The killer had been clever enough to stay wide of plowed ground. Gabe couldn't determine what direction the killer rode after leaving the live oaks; the rocky land was simply too hard to reveal any sign.

He gave up after a couple of hours of fruitless search and rode back to the barn. Bonnie Cummings was inside, kneeling beside her husband. She had draped a blanket over the body. She watched Gabe approach with red-rimmed eyes.

"I can't find any tracks," he said.

She accepted the news in silence.

"I can send Roy Culpepper out," he went on. "He does a little undertaking on the side."

Bonnie shook her head against it. "I'll dress him up in his best overalls," she whispered. "If you wouldn't mind, ask Carl Jones if he'll dig the grave. We ain't got the money to pay him just now, but we'll have a few pigs to sell early in the spring."

"I'll talk to Carl," he told her gently, "after I question Buck Ramsey as to his whereabouts. I'm gonna need some evidence before Judge Green will issue an arrest warrant for Ramsey. I'm afraid it isn't enough that Ramsey pulled a gun on Clarence yesterday."

"I know he's the one who done it," Bonnie said, after giving Gabe a questioning look, before gazing down at her dead husband. "I just know it was him. Clarence never did have no enemies. He was always kind to everybody."

Gabe nodded. "I never heard anybody say a bad word about him. I'm real sorry about what happened, Miz Cummings. Maybe you oughta send a letter to Bobby over at Waco . . . tell him about his pa, and that he's needed back home now."

Bonnie closed her eyes briefly. "Never did learn how to read or write," she said.

"I'll see that Bobby gets word," he said, "if you can remember the name of that gin where he works."

"Thompson's," she replied. "Clarence told me it was right close to the Brazos."

Gabe turned to leave. "Be seeing you, Miz Cummings. Let me know if there's anything I can do, like helping with chores until Bobby comes."

She managed a weak smile. "I've still got my girls left. We'll get by."

109

He walked out of the barn to mount the mule, his thoughts now turned to the forthcoming meeting with Ramsey, the questions he must ask. Since the gunman first showed up around Eagle Springs, Gabe had known something like this was likely to happen. Gabe couldn't remember when the last shooting took place in this end of the county. A few years back, someone found an old-timer named Windy Brown lying along a deserted stretch of the Leon River with a pistol clamped in his fist and a bullet hole in his skull. It was concluded Windy shot himself not long after his wife's death from pneumonia. Harlan Huffman remembered how the old man grieved over it. There hadn't been an honest-to-goodness killing here since the war.

He started the mule toward town, thinking how right he'd been to worry over Buck Ramsey showing up. Sometimes a gut feeling proved reliable. It could hardly be called coincidence that a murder occurred as soon as a notorious gunman came to town. It fell to Gabe to prove that the two were connected.

When he rode to Main Street and started through town, Thelma Culpepper hailed him from the front porch of the mercantile where she'd been sweeping. Halting the mule, Gabe leaned out of the saddle.

"Ask Roy to drive out to the Cummings

place," he told her. "Clarence was killed early this morning, and I imagine Bonnie could use some help with the body."

Thelma almost dropped her broom. "Killed? In the Lord's name, how did it happen?"

"Someone shot him, Miz Culpepper," he replied. "There weren't any witnesses."

The woman's face lost most of its color. She swung a glance toward the creek. "It has to be that stranger who rode into town the other day, saying he's Johnny Ramsey's brother. Carl Jones told my husband that he's been hanging around down at the saloon, and that he just got out of prison. Who else would harm a peaceful farmer like Clarence Cummings? One has to wonder why he'd pick Clarence . . ."

"I'm headed down to talk to Ramsey now," Gabe confided. "For the time being, I don't have any proof that Ramsey did it."

"Nothing else makes good sense," Thelma said. "I'll tell Roy what happened. I'm sure he won't mind lending Bonnie and the children a hand. They owe us for a bill of goods, but Roy never pressed Clarence about it. He would have paid if he was able. Nearly everybody felt sorry for them lately, what with no rain, and cotton won't sell."

Gabe tipped his hat to the woman and

started the mule away from the store, looking for smoke from Ramsey's fire. In spite of the chill, there was no smoke coming from the creekbank, leaving Gabe to wonder if he'd find the camp empty again.

South of town, he caught a glimpse of the roan gelding, standing hipshot beneath a cottonwood tree near the tent. "He's there," Gabe whispered to himself, unconsciously touching the butt of the pistol on his hip.

Ramsey heard the mule and walked away from the tree, where it appeared he'd been saddling his horse. When he saw Gabe, he stood rock-still without opening his coat to get at his gun.

He doesn't act worried, Gabe thought. He rode up to Ramsey and pulled back on the reins. "I need to ask you some questions," he began, watching the gunman's expression closely.

"Ask. I was just leavin'," Ramsey said. There was no inflection in his voice, as though he didn't care about the questions either way.

"Where were you early this morning? Just before daylight."

"Right here," the gunman replied, aiming a thumb at his tent. "Why'd you ask?"

"Somebody shot Clarence Cummings right before daybreak," Gabe continued. "I saw you out there yesterday, if you'll remember."

Ramsey's face did not change. "That don't make me the one who pulled the trigger," he sad flatly. "I talked to Cummings a minute or two. He acted jumpy when I asked about him seein' a wagon come out of that dry wash the night my brother was killed. You said yourself he could be lyin'."

"I was told you pulled a gun on Clarence yesterday."

Ramsey's eyes got noticeably narrower. "Whoever told you that is a lyin' son of a bitch," he said, his voice turned hard. "When I draw this Colt, I'll damn sure use it. Somebody's tryin' to frame me. Who told you I pulled a gun on that farmer?"

Gabe considered the wisdom of telling Ramsey what Peggy Sue told him. "Right now, that ain't what matters. Besides, it's just your word that you were here this morning and that you didn't draw on Clarence the day before. It's my job to investigate what happened out there. I'll ask the questions."

For a moment, Gabe wondered if he'd pushed Ramsey too far. Ramsey bit down hard, though he held his tongue. Gabe gave the blue roan a close examination, looking for dried lather on its coat, or any sign that it had been ridden hard recently. "Your horse don't appear traveled, like you rode back to town in a hurry. I'm gonna check into that story, that you questioned Clarence at gunpoint. But I'm advising you not to leave town, Mr. Ramsey. Not until I know who did the shooting out at the Cummings farm."

The gunman seemed mildly amused. "Wasn't plannin' to leave anyway," he said, then his eyelids slitted, the amusement gone.

Gabe straightened a little in the saddle. "What I said just now wasn't friendly advice. I'll have Judge Green issue a warrant for your arrest if you leave without my permission."

Gabe knew he was on uncertain ground with a dangerous man, but he wasn't about to back off, even at the risk of losing his own life. The people of Eagle Springs had voted him into office as sheriff and he couldn't let them down. A local citizen was dead by violence and Gabe fully intended to find out who the killer was, even if it meant facing up to the challenge of a notorious gunfighter.

Ramsey stared at him with those piercing blue eyes, then he gave a slight nod.

"I'll let you have your way — for now," he said. "I'll give you a fair amount of time. Just remember, I came here to find out who shot my brother — I won't let anything stand in my way."

Gabe had started to pull the mule toward town when he heard Ramsey speak again.

"The old woman knows what happened to

Johnny. I figure she also knows why my ma left so sudden-like."

Gabe frowned, glancing over his shoulder at Clara's house. "You heard what she said when I asked her about it. I won't stick a gun in her face just to see if she knows any more."

The gunman's gaze fell to Gabe's waist. "I see you're wearin' a pistol now," he remarked coldly. "I reckon you think you need it on account of me."

Gabe took a deep breath, feeling the beginnings of fear when he heard the tone Ramsey used. "I suppose that's the truth of it," he answered, watching Ramsey's gun hand, then his face when Ramsey's coat remained closed.

"Makes it my turn to give you some friendly advice, Sheriff," he said slowly, his voice thickening with menace. "Think on it real hard before you draw that gun against me. I'll kill you if you go for your gun. You've got my word on it."

Gabe knew he couldn't ride away after a remark like that, neither did he want to push the man too far. "I've got no doubts that you're faster, Mr. Ramsey," he replied carefully, determined not to let his fear show, no matter what the gunman said. "But I've got a job to do for the folks in this town, and

I aim to do it any way I can. I won't run off and hide someplace if the time comes when I have to arrest you."

Ramsey appeared to accept what Gabe said. "I didn't shoot the farmer. If you've got any sense, you'll figure out somebody's tryin' to frame me. I'd have to be plumb crazy to kill a man and wait right here for the law to come after me. If I'd killed him, I'd have hightailed it out of town."

Gabe was forced to think about it. "Seems like you would," he agreed. "Maybe you think I'm just plain dumb. Or scared of you."

"I wouldn't be very smart to hang around. You could send for the Texas Rangers if you were afraid to face me alone."

"I suppose I could," Gabe answered, "if you scared me, which you ain't. I'm not looking to get myself killed for a fifteen-dollar-a-month job, but I'm not afraid to arrest the man who shot Clarence. When I know the killer's identity, I'll put irons on him and take him to the Gatesville jail, if I'm able."

Ramsey nodded, to say he took Gabe's word. "Somebody's tryin' to play both of us for a fool," he went on, a hint of anger returning to his voice, "making me look like a killer, so you'll arrest me. I say that's proof my brother was shot by some yellow bastard who still lives around here, worryin' that I'll

116

find out who he is."

Ramsey's logic made some sense. "Maybe," Gabe told him. "Things could have happened that way, until you get to looking for a reason why anybody would kill Johnny in the first place. That's the part I can't figure."

Ramsey looked past Gabe just then, at the back of Clara Hawkins's house. "Yonder lives somebody who knows," he said, sounding absolutely certain of it. "That old woman saw what happened and she's been keepin' it quiet. I intend to find out who she's tryin' to protect. Or who it is she's afraid of."

Gabe pondered it briefly. "I can't think of a soul she'd be scared of. Nobody around here would do her any harm. Same goes for trying to protect somebody. I haven't got the slightest notion who that could be. She's hardly got any friends. Folks didn't think much of the way she used to make a living, taking in laundry before the war."

Ramsey's eyes were still on the house. "Where does she get her money now?" he asked.

"I've got no idea," Gabe replied. "I suppose she saved a little. She lives out of her garden mostly. Every now and then she buys a little sugar and flour. I could ask over at the store. Maybe Harlan or his wife knows where she gets the money to buy staples, although I can't

117

see how it matters."

"Maybe it don't," Ramsey said, watching Gabe now. "The old gent who used to be sheriff is hidin' something too. I can see it in his eyes."

"Could be he's only got a guess," Gabe argued. "I've always regarded Harvey as an honest man. I can't think of anybody who wouldn't agree. If he knew for sure who killed your brother, he'd have charged him with murder. Harvey may have his suspicions, but I'd nearly swear he don't know for certain who the killer is."

"I said I'd give you a fair amount of time," the gunman said. "But if you don't come up with some answers, I'm gonna start looking for myself, and I damn sure won't let anybody give me the runaround."

Gabe didn't like it when Ramsey handed out ultimatums like that, and he summoned the nerve to say so. "I won't let you tell me how to do my job, Mr. Ramsey, and I won't let you push folks around here, either. Right now, you're still the prime suspect in the murder of Clarence Cummings. Your reputation makes you the only suspect I've got."

"I didn't do it," Ramsey declared, "and nobody's gonna frame me for it."

"Everybody in this end of the county will be after me to arrest you for killing Clarence,"

Gabe replied. "But I won't do it, not till I know for sure that you're guilty. Remember what I said — don't try to leave town or I'll put the Rangers on your trail."

Ramsey grunted. "You can count on one thing, Sheriff Miller — I won't be leavin' this town until I get what I came after." He turned his back on Gabe and walked to his horse.

Gabe was left with the feeling that Ramsey meant every word of what he just said. Aiming the mule for the road to Gatesville, Gabe started on the journey to deliver payment for a dead man's taxes, wishing he'd never heard of a gunfighter named Buck Ramsey.

CHAPTER 11

The rocky road winding its way to the county seat was harder on the mule's hooves than Gabe expected. Riding up to the big stone courthouse at the center of the city square, he felt the mule travel a bit tender-footed. He tied off in the shade of a big pecan tree and headed up the steps to Judge Green's office. After his meeting with the judge, he meant to stop by the Gatesville sheriff's office. Sheriff Troy Lee Hunt had countywide jurisdiction, and it seemed a wise move to let him know about the arrival of Buck Ramsey and the murder of Clarence Cummings.

He found the judge in his office and pulled off his hat when he entered the room. "Afternoon, Judge," he said while approaching the desk with the envelope in his hands. "Here's the tax money owed by Clarence Cummings."

Judge Green passed a fleshy palm over his bald head before he took the envelope. In his sixties, more than a hundred pounds overweight, he seldom showed any excitement or agitation. "Glad he's current now," the judge remarked. "I'll make out a receipt you can take back to him."

"I'm afraid he won't be needing it now," Gabe replied, sighing. "Somebody shot him dead early this morning. I can take the receipt to his wife."

Judge Green's eyebrows arched, reminding Gabe of crawling inchworms.

"Do you know who did it?" he asked.

"Only a suspicion, for now. A stranger arrived in Eagle Springs the other day, a man fresh out of prison. His name is Buck Ramsey, and he claims to be looking for the man who killed his younger brother ten years back while he was gone to the war. I've got no proof Ramsey killed Mr. Cummings, but I'm working on it."

"I take it there weren't any witnesses," the judge said. He gave Gabe a cursory look of appraisal. "I'd tell Troy Hunt about it while you're in Gatesville. Not that you can't handle it by yourself, Gabriel. But you'll admit that you don't have much experience with this sort of crime."

Gabe nodded. "I'd planned to talk to Sheriff Hunt about what happened, soon as I gave you this money. It's true I don't have any experience solving a murder. It makes things worse to have a gunfighter like Ramsey for a suspect. If I can prove a case against him, I'm not looking forward to placing him under arrest."

"You say he's a gunfighter?"

"Harvey remembers him," Gabe replied. "He told me Ramsey was one of Quantrill's raiders — then he rode with Bloody Bill Anderson for a time."

Judge Green scowled. "Nobody on earth any worse than Bill Anderson. Him and his bunch weren't worth the gunpowder it took to kill them. If this Ramsey fellow was a part of Bloody Bill's gang, I'd give him a wide berth as long as I could. If you can prove your case against him, send for Troy and his deputy. I'd advise against trying to take him alone. You're too young to know what some of those old-time gunslicks were like. The biggest part of them got hanged, or sent to prison. Times aren't quite as wild as they used to be, and nearly everybody in this county is glad of it."

Judge Green began writing out a receipt for the taxes. Gabe looked absently out the office window until the paper was filled out, wondering if he'd ever be able to prove Ramsey did the killing. On the ride to Gatesville he'd had plenty of time to think of ways he meant to go about it. Ramsey was as cool a customer as Gabe had ever seen. He appeared to be completely unruffled by Gabe's questions. Still, some of what Ramsey said was beginning to make more sense. If he'd killed Clarence, then why was he still hanging around, running the risk of arrest?

"Here's the receipt," Judge Green said, handing it across the desk. "I don't suppose there's been any rain over your way to take some of the strain off the farmers?"

"Not a drop," he answered. "Cotton prices are so low that none of us can afford to sell what we made last year. It looks like only a fool would raise more cotton, only that land isn't much good for anything else."

The judge's expression turned thoughtful. "Except for the good bottomland northeast, belonging to Cleveland Wade. He owns the best grazing."

Gabe shook his head as he pocketed the receipt. "He's the one who loaned Clarence Cummings the tax money, on account of they were neighbors, I suppose. Folks who know him claim he's real generous to his friends."

Judge Green seemed doubtful. "That's not the impression he gave me when he came to this county. Surprises the hell out of me that he'd loan a poor farmer any money. I had Wade pegged for a greedy man. I never did feel like I ought to trust him."

"He's real boastful," Gabe agreed. "Sometimes he acts like he owns the whole town. He backed another candidate for our sheriff's election. I won the job by a whisker."

The judge's expression softened. "Some folks worried that you were too young, Gabriel. As far as I'm concerned, you've always done your duties real well. But I'd still recommend that you tell Troy what's going on, just in case you need some help with that Ramsey fellow."

Gabe nodded and walked out of the office and down the stairs to the street. Across the square, he sighted the sheriff's office and started toward it, facing a chilly wind.

When he walked in, he found Troy Hunt warming his backside at a potbelly stove. The sheriff smiled when he saw Gabe.

"If it ain't Sheriff Gabriel Miller," he said, offering a handshake. "How're things in the east end of the county?"

"Not as good as they might be," Gabe answered. "We had a killing early this morning. A farmer by the name of Clarence Cummings was shot dead in his hay barn, along about sunrise."

Hunt's face grew serious. "Any idea who did it?"

"Only a suspect, for now. A stranger showed up the other day, fresh out of Yuma prison. His name is Buck Ramsey. Harvey told me he's a dangerous man."

The sheriff's eyes narrowed. "I've heard plenty about Buck Ramsey. Harvey's damn sure right about him bein' dangerous. I had Buck figured for dead. Hadn't heard of him in quite a long spell."

"He was at Yuma, so Harvey said. He came back to Eagle Springs to find out who killed his twelve-year-old brother while he was off to the war."

"I remember that shooting," Hunt recalled. "Me an' Harvey talked about it plenty of times. The boy's mother disappeared the same time. Harvey never figured out who could have killed the boy, or why the woman took off the way she did."

Gabe nodded once. "I was looking into it, trying to help Buck Ramsey follow a mighty cold trail, when Clarence got shot. Now Ramsey is the only suspect I've got. I saw him out near the Cummings farm the day before. Harvey told us that was where he lost the tracks of Miz Ramsey's wagon, ten years ago. I figure Buck Ramsey has to be the only one with any kind of motive for Clarence's death. I was told he questioned Clarence at gunpoint about what he might have seen or heard the night his ma drove her wagon past the Cummings place."

Hunt watched Gabe closely. "I'm sure you

125

asked Buck where he was at the time of the shooting."

"He claims he was at his camp down on Justin Creek. He told me he'd have to be plain stupid to hang around town if he was the one who killed Clarence. Just thinking about it, what he says makes a heck of a lot of sense to me."

By the look on the sheriff's face, he wasn't satisfied. "Some characters think they're so tough they don't have to run from the law."

Gabe rocked back on his boot heels, remembering Ramsey's threat. "He told me he'd kill me if I came after him with a gun to haul him to jail. He made it real plain he'd shoot me, rather than go."

Hunt glanced to a rifle rack on the back wall of his office. "If the time comes you've got enough evidence to arrest him, me an' my deputy will come over, armed to the teeth. Even a sure enough bad hombre won't try his hand against three armed men, not unless he's loco."

"I'll let you know," Gabe said, turning for the door.

"How's ol' Harvey doin'?" Hunt asked.

"It's bad. I don't figure he'll last much longer. He can't hardly get out of bed now."

"Shame," the sheriff said, eyes downcast, as though remembering Harvey. "I'll ride

126

over, next time I get the chance. Harvey Barnes was a good lawman. Only thing he ever did that stuck in my craw was caterin' to that rich bastard, the one who bought up half the county."

"Cleve Wade," Gabe muttered, then he looked at Sheriff Hunt. "I never did hear of Harvey having much to do with Cleve . . ."

Hunt aimed a thoughtful stare at the wall. "He acted like he'd be willin' to shine Wade's boots a few years back. I suppose that was before your time, Gabriel. Before you married that yellow-haired beauty from Eagle Springs." He looked back at Gabe. "Give my best to Martha. My wife asks about her from time to time. Tell your wife we both said hello."

"I'll do it," Gabe said. He waved to Sheriff Hunt and walked out.

On the way over to the mule, he tried to decide where he should continue with the investigation into Clarence's death. How could he tie Ramsey to the shooting? There wasn't any real evidence linking Ramsey to the murder. Finding Ramsey close to the Cummings farm and hearing Peggy Sue's account of a hearsay threat simply weren't enough to go on.

He boarded the mule to ride back to Eagle Springs with a remark by Sheriff Hunt rattling around inside his head. Gabe would never have figured Harvey catering to Cleve Wade, even if he was the richest man in town. Harvey wasn't like that, so why did the Gatesville sheriff remember him acting that way? Maybe Martha would know . . .

Fierce gusts of wind rattled loose window-panes while Martha prepared supper. Just after dark the wind picked up, turning colder, but there was no hint of rain. Gabe added mesquite wood to the fireplace. Delicious smells came from the cookstove as Martha pan-fried deer steaks from the buck he'd killed this fall.

"I wouldn't say Harvey behaved much differently toward Cleveland Wade," Martha said, answering Gabe's question after a silence. "What makes you ask?"

Gabe watched the flames a moment, warming his hands. "It was something Sheriff Hunt said, that Harvey catered to Cleve and it used to stick in his craw for Harvey to warm up to a rich man."

"Plenty of folks go out of their way to be nice to the Wade family," Martha said. "It's natural for people to treat rich folks different. Darn near every boy in these parts acted real cordial to Peggy Sue, but that's because she's so pretty."

"Not near as pretty as you," he told her, admiring his wife's good looks from the fireplace.

She looked over her shoulder and smiled at him. "Aren't you being sweet tonight, Mr. Miller." Now she stirred the strips of deer meat again. "Have you found a way to prove it was Buck Ramsey who shot Clarence Cummings?"

Staring at the fire, he said, "No. I don't know where to begin. Ramsey says he didn't do it. And he claims he didn't pull a gun on Clarence yesterday. He thinks I oughta know somebody is trying to frame him. One thing he said made sense to me: If he'd been the one to shoot Clarence, he would have cleared out of Coryell County instead of sitting down there by the creek until I found him." He didn't tell Martha that Ramsey also said he'd kill Gabe if he tried to arrest him — no point in worrying her.

"If you believe him," Martha continued, "that somebody is trying to frame him, then who could it possibly be?"

"That's just it," Gabe replied, his mouth watering, thinking about the taste of deer steak fried with onions. "Who would have a reason for wanting Ramsey out of the way?"

Martha looked at him again, no longer smiling. "That's easy enough — whoever killed

Johnny Ramsey. If Buck Ramsey is right, it means Johnny's killer is someone who lives around here, and now he's worried that he'll be discovered."

Gabe chewed his bottom lip absently. "Ramsey said the same thing."

A moment later, Martha left the stove to come over to the fireplace. She looked into Gabe's eyes, wiping her hands on her apron. "A lot of people will be clamoring for Buck Ramsey's arrest when they hear what happened to Clarence. You know how folks talk. By tomorrow, nearly everybody will know. They'll be coming to you, wanting to know why you haven't arrested Ramsey."

"I 'spect they will," he told her. He'd been thinking about it on the ride back from Gatesville. "But the truth is, I don't have a shred of real evidence against him."

"Some won't like it, if you let him stay out of jail," she said, worry pinching her brow. "You're the elected sheriff and they'll expect you to do something."

"I know," he whispered. He kissed her lightly on the mouth. "But I can't arrest him without being able to prove he did it. The way things are now, I can't prove a thing. I've got strong suspicions that Ramsey tried to make Clarence tell him what he saw the night Johnny was killed, his ma's wagon passing by, and maybe who was with her. The trouble is, that's only a guess."

A thought occurred to Martha — he could see it on her face in the firelight.

"Clara Hawkins may be the only one who actually knows what happened the night Johnny was killed," she said. "Living so close, she might have seen something. If I was sheriff, I'd start with Clara. Solving that puzzle, even if it did happen ten years ago, will take you straight to the doorstep of the man who killed Clarence Cummings."

He didn't need any extra time to know how right Martha was. Finding a killer who remained hidden for ten years, as impossible as it seemed now, was the only logical place to begin.

CHAPTER 12

A thin layer of ice greeted him early that morning when he went to the shed to feed and water the pigs. All night long the wind howled around the corners of the house. The ride to town numbed his hands and feet. He got a fire started in the potbelly at the office and waited for the room to warm, remembering the plumes of smoke coming from stovepipes all across town as he'd ridden across the ridge. Smoke curled above Ramsey's camp too, sufficient proof that the gunman was still around. It still puzzled Gabe, why Ramsey stayed if he'd been the one to kill Clarence. More and more now, Gabe was becoming convinced that Ramsey wasn't the killer. Ramsey wouldn't risk bringing the law down on him as he searched for his brother's murderer. It was beginning to look more and more like someone was trying to frame Ramsey, to get him out of the way.

He heard boots coming down the boardwalk. Harlan Huffman passed the office window to open the door.

"Mornin', Gabe," Harlan said, closing the door behind him.

Gabe could tell there was something on Harlan's mind. He said, "Good morning," waiting for the storekeeper to get to the purpose behind his visit.

Harlan walked over to the stove, warming his hands. "I was wonderin' when you intend to arrest that Ramsey feller," he began. "Folks kept askin' me and Hope why Buck Ramsey wasn't headed over to the county jail. So I decided I'd better ask you about your intentions."

Gabe knew Martha had rightly predicted what the townspeople would want. "I don't have enough evidence against Ramsey for Judge Green to issue a warrant."

Harlan's eyes clouded. "Hell's fire, Gabe. A blind man can see it was Ramsey who shot Clarence. This stranger shows up, right out of prison, so I hear, an' then Clarence gets killed in his own barn, right after he tells Cleve Wade that Ramsey stuck a gun under his chin. How much more proof do you need?"

"A judge would call it hearsay evidence," Gabe argued, wagging his head. "Hearing what Clarence told Cleve isn't enough to convict a man for murder."

The look on Harlan's face said he wasn't

satisfied. "What are you gonna do about it? Surely you ain't gonna let Ramsey get off scot-free."

"I intend to find out who did it, Harlan. I can't just toss a man in jail without any proof. There weren't any witnesses to the shooting. The way things are now, my hands are tied. I talked to Judge Green about it yesterday. I've got to come up with something that will stick in a court of law."

Harlan scowled. "Some folks ain't gonna be too happy to hear it, when you don't arrest Ramsey. There'll be talk that maybe you aren't doin' your job. The taxpayers are payin' your salary, remember. Most are gonna want some sort of action."

"I'll do everything I can to put the finger on whoever did the shooting," Gabe replied. "Right now, all I've been able to come up with are a bunch of dead ends. Ramsey claims he stayed around his camp all night. I'm hoping I can come up with a witness who'll say otherwise. Miz Hawkins is about the best bet to have seen Ramsey leave, if she happened to be awake. Maybe she can tell me something. Which reminds me about a question I needed to ask. Where does Clara get the money to buy sugar and flour? She could hardly have saved enough doing laundry to live the rest of her life, could she?"

Harlan had his answer ready. "Cleveland Wade helps her out from time to time, a few dollars here an' there. He told me he feels sorry for her, livin' all alone, without no pension. I say we're real lucky to have a man like Cleve around here."

"There's no denying he's generous," Gabe agreed. "Like when he loaned Clarence the money for his back taxes. Hard to say why he does that sort of thing. Being neighborly, I suppose, even if Clara isn't exactly his neighbor."

"He's liable to be the one makin' the most noise if you don't put Buck Ramsey behind bars," Harlan warned.

Gabe shook his head. "He can talk to Judge Green about it, if he cares to. According to the law, I can't arrest Ramsey without some proof that he's guilty."

"There's some who figure you're scared of Ramsey," Harlan continued. "You know how folks like to gossip."

"I'd be crazy if I wasn't a little bit afraid of a man with Ramsey's reputation," Gabe said. "Harvey told me Ramsey is a professional gunman, and to be careful around him. But if I can prove he killed Clarence Cummings, I'll place him under arrest. Sheriff Hunt promised he'd come over if I figured I needed any help with it."

Harlan looked away, gazing out the window. "I'd hate to see you look bad in front of the voters who elected you. You'll have to run for office again in three more years. I'm not tellin' you what you oughta do, but maybe you need to think about how it's gonna look if you let Ramsey stay on the loose."

"I already explained why I can't lock him up," Gabe told him sincerely, wishing Harlan would let it rest. "I know some folks are likely to grumble, but they'll have to understand that I have to get my hands on some solid proof before the judge will give me a warrant. If I hauled Ramsey over to Gatesville without evidence to convict him, Judge Green would have to let him go."

It seemed Harlan finally accepted the news. He gave a silent nod and started across the room. "Be seein' you, Gabe," he said, without turning around. "I sure hope you find what you're looking for, before somebody else gets killed."

Gabe watched the storekeeper walk out, feeling helpless. As soon as the door closed, he shook his head. How can I make him and everybody else understand, he wondered.

Later, when the stove had made the room comfortable, he walked over to the desk and slumped in his chair, wondering where to begin the investigation. It was unlikely that

Clara Hawkins saw Ramsey leave camp in the dark on the night Clarence was shot. And it was just as sure a bet that she hadn't heard anything, either. Down deep, Gabe had begun to believe Ramsey's version of events that night. There was no logical reason for Ramsey to want Clarence out of the way. Who except Johnny Ramsey's killer would think a peace-loving farmer posed a threat? In order to find out why Clarence was shot, Gabe would have to unravel a ten-year-old mystery.

Gabe toyed with a sheaf of papers, his mind on other things. Harlan had given him one bit of news, the source of Clara Hawkins's meager income. Gabe couldn't quite believe that Cleveland Wade was such a generous man, to hand out money the way he did.

When he couldn't come up with any answers that satisfied him, he glanced at a tintype of Martha that sat atop the desk. Seeing Martha's likeness reminded him that Christmas was less than a week away. He'd already picked out presents for her down at the mercantile, a bolt of bright yellow cloth so she could make a new dress. If only he had enough money, he would get her a store-bought dress. But with his cotton unsold he would have barely enough for the material and some matching ribbon for her hair, perhaps one of those little bottles of rose-scented perfume he'd had his eye on

137

the last time he was at Roy's. Martha would look so pretty in a new yellow dress when they went to church on Sundays. Almost everybody in Preacher Sims's congregation stared at her. Gabe knew he was the envy of most every man around Eagle Springs for having a wife like Martha. He counted himself lucky, when he thought about it. In the spring and summer, when the congregation held a picnic lunch on the church grounds after the preaching, Gabe couldn't help but notice how everyone looked at his wife. He often wished he had the money to give her a better life.

"What am I doing?" he asked himself, awakening from his daydream with a start. "I've got a murder to solve, two of them, in fact. Why am I just sitting here?"

He stood up and closed the flue in the stovepipe, bent on asking Clara a few more questions. Perhaps Ramsey was right, that Clara knew more than she was willing to say about the night Johnny died. Gabe had gotten the same sense when he questioned her, that there was something she didn't want to talk about. Buttoning his coat, he walked out into an icy wind and locked the door. Off to the south of town, smoke rose from the chimney atop Clara's house. Perhaps if he yelled loud enough, the old woman would understand that he wouldn't give up until he got some answers from her, answers that satisfied him.

Walking along Main Street, it struck him how unlikely Eagle Springs was for a pair of unsolved murders and the disappearance of a victim's mother. A half dozen stores and shops lined the single street through town. It was the quiet sort of place where nothing was supposed to happen, a good place to raise crops and children, get to know your neighbors, live in peace. The most excitement in town was the fall ginning of cotton, after the first frost had killed the plants so the bowls could be picked easily. Everyone gathered around the gin when the cotton wagons came to town, talking about the weather, the size of the cotton and corn crop, the price of beef on the hoof. The community was simply too small to harbor a murderer who could conceal his identity. In an area where folks knew each other most of their lives, someone capable of cold-blooded murder should stand out from the rest. A killer wouldn't be able to stalk his victim without attracting the attention of a local citizen or two. Gabe knew someone had probably seen whoever was responsible for both crimes. What would keep them from talking? What was the value of their silence?

"Ramsey didn't kill Clarence," he whispered, hunkered down inside his coat collar to keep the wind from his neck, quickening his strides toward Clara's house. "He's too smart to make a target of himself like that, no matter what he thought Clarence might be keeping from him." Gabe reasoned that even if Ramsey had Clarence figured for his brother's killer, which was the most unlikely prospect Gabe could think of, Ramsey would have taken his revenge and then ridden off for parts unknown. He wouldn't have stayed around Eagle Springs. His camp down at the creek would be empty now.

Gabe sighted the widow's house and swung south. Farther down the creek, he glimpsed Ramsey's army tent and his blue roan. He's waiting to see what I come up with, Gabe thought. No telling what he'll do if I come up empty.

At Clara's front door, he knocked loudly. A few moments passed before he heard the sound of her walking stick on the floor. A latch rattled, then Clara peered out, wrapped in a heavy woolen shawl.

"It's you," she said, sounding unhappy about Gabe's appearance on her doorstep. She looked him up and down. "I hope you haven't come back to ask me silly questions. I told you everything I remember."

"May I come in, Miz Hawkins?" he asked.

Though she seemed uncomfortable, she nodded and opened the door to admit him.

"I'm really quite busy," she said, raising her voice so she could hear herself. "I was knitting."

"This won't take long," he replied, pulling off his hat, walking down a musty hallway to the back room of the tiny house. The floorboards creaked under his weight. He saw old furniture in the single bedroom: a battered chest of drawers and a sagging four-poster bed. A rusted Franklin stove gave off heat in a rear corner of the house where an empty rocking chair sat. Faded green curtains kept out sunlight. The place had a look of neglect about it.

Clara came behind him, pecking the floor with her cane. "You may sit over there," she said, pointing to a hidebound wooden chair. She hobbled to her rocker in a pair of well-worn high button shoes.

Gabe settled into the chair. Its rawhide bindings protested, cracking when he sat down. On a wall behind Clara's rocker was a dusty tintype of a man in a black broadcloth suit, her husband, Gabe supposed. "Clarence Cummings was killed yesterday," he began, watching the old woman's face for her reaction. "He was shot, and I believe it has something to do with the murder of Johnny Ramsey."

"Goodness me!" Clara exclaimed, covering

her mouth with a wrinkled hand, her rheumy eyes fixed on Gabe. "Poor Clarence, and now his wife has so many children to raise alone." She swallowed, then her glance went to a rear window overlooking Justin Creek. "It was that tall man who did it," she said, lowering her voice. "The one who's camped over there, the fellow with those odd-colored eyes."

"Johnny Ramsey's brother?" Gabe explained. "I don't think he's the one who shot Clarence. He came back to Eagle Springs to find out who killed Johnny and to see if he can learn where his ma went."

Clara's gaze drifted back to Gabe, and he was sure something was making her wary.

"The older boy's name was Buck," she said. "Doesn't look like him, best I remember. They didn't live here long. Of course, you wouldn't know that, being from Leon Junction."

"I was told, Miz Hawkins. It would be a big help if you could remember anything about the night Johnny was killed. Anything at all."

She moved her head from side to side. "I must have been sound asleep when it happened," she replied, unconsciously clasping her hands together in her lap as she began to rock the chair. "If I'd heard or seen anything, I would have told Harvey about it."

Gabe let out a sigh of frustration. "The Ramseys' old house is mighty close to yours, Miz Hawkins. I don't see how you could have missed hearing the gunshot that killed Johnny."

Clara stiffened a little in her chair. "Are you implying that I'm not telling the truth, young man?"

"No, ma'am," Gabe protested, spreading his palms in a helpless gesture. "I'm only saying that maybe you forgot to mention something to Sheriff Barnes. It's real easy to be forgetful. It happens to me all the time."

The old woman pushed herself up from the rocker, her arms a bit unsteady. She pointed a trembling finger at her front door. "Get out!" she cried, as the beginnings of tears formed in her eyes. "I won't have you calling me a liar in my own house!"

He got out of the chair. "That isn't what I said, Miz Hawkins. You might have forgotten something, a detail you thought was too small to mention."

She took a yellowed handkerchief from a pocket of her dress to dab her cheeks. "I want you to get out of my house," she said, fighting back more tears. "I don't want you to ever come back. I'm an old woman. Please leave me alone."

CHAPTER 13

During lunch, he told Martha about his visit with Clara Hawkins. "She acted frightened. She ordered me out of her house. Something I said made her start crying."

Martha shook her head, daintily chewing a bite of ham.

"She gets a little income from Cleve Wade," he said thoughtfully. "Harlan told me it isn't much, barely enough for sugar and flour. Cleve feels sorry for her, living all alone without any kind of pension. It don't hardly seem like enough so she'd protect Cleve, if he happened to be Johnny's murderer."

"I can't believe Cleveland Wade would do such a thing. Why would the richest man in the county run the risk of shooting a boy Johnny's age? What would he stand to gain?"

"I've been thinking the same thing myself," Gabe replied. "There's no motive. But when I try to find a motive that fits anyone else around here for shooting a twelve-year-old boy, I always come up short. That's the hardest part, when you try to solve this murder. Who would have a reason to kill the boy?"

"Unless Johnny saw something he wasn't supposed to see," Martha went on. "The best explanation is that Johnny witnessed some terrible thing and his killer needed his silence."

"What could he have seen?" Gabe asked, after cleaning his plate of the last scrap of food. "No crime was committed before the boy died, not that anybody remembers."

A carriage was waiting for Gabe when he got back to the office. Cleveland Wade was sitting on the driver's seat, watching Gabe dismount at the hitchrail. Cleve was a powerfully built man in his mid-fifties, Gabe guessed, with a shock of red hair like his daughter's across his forehead, held in place by the tall crown of a Stetson hat. His square jaw was set, his mouth in a hard line, when Gabe walked over to the carriage.

"Afternoon, Mr. Wade," Gabe said, extending his hand.

Cleve ignored the offer of a handshake, fixing Gabe with a steely look. "Why hasn't Buck Ramsey been arrested?" he asked sharply, working his hands around the reins to the buggy horse.

"I've got no proof that he killed Clarence," Gabe replied, letting his hand fall to his side.

145

"I need some evidence, an eyewitness, someone who saw Ramsey near the Cummings farm on the morning Clarence was shot. I intend to ask around. Maybe someone got a glimpse of Ramsey, if he's truly the one who did it."

"Of course he did it," Cleve snapped, sounding even more irritated. "If you had a lick of sense, you'd know that already and you'd have that killer behind bars."

"I don't have enough for Judge Green to issue the warrant," Gabe protested, disliking the way Cleve regarded him, with what could only be called contempt. "You can talk to the judge yourself if you have any doubts."

The rancher let out an impatient sigh. "I warned everyone that you were too damn young to hold down a peace officer's job."

Gabe bristled a little over the remark. He stood his ground and looked Cleve in the eye. "I'm more than able to do whatever is within the authority of my badge. I can't bring charges against Ramsey without proof. If I can find evidence to prove him guilty, I'll take him to jail."

Cleve let his impatience show again, fingering the reins while shaking his head. "I 'spect there'll be a bunch of voters who'll be sorry they cast a ballot for you if Buck Ramsey's still a free man come nightfall. Honest citizens in this town are gonna demand you arrest that hired gun." He aimed a glance in the direction of the Gatesville road. "I believe I'll drive over to have a word with Judge Green about this matter. Maybe he can make you understand that you've got a duty to protect the taxpayers around here."

Before Gabe could say more, Cleve slapped the reins over the buggy horse's rump and drove off in a cloud of dust. Gabe watched the carriage roll away, gritting his teeth. The rancher meant to bully him into arresting Ramsey without a shred of evidence to prove a case against him. "You don't own me, Cleve," he said under his breath, wishing he'd remembered to ask the rancher what Clarence said about Ramsey pulling a gun. Cleve wasn't in the right mood just then to ask, Gabe decided as the carriage sped out of sight down the Gatesville road.

He climbed the boardwalk to unlock the office door and noticed a hopeful looking bank of dark clouds along the northern horizon. With the temperature near freezing, the clouds were likely to drop sleet or snow. Any form of moisture would be welcomed by the farmers and ranchers around Eagle Springs. Even hailstones the size of cannonballs would eventually melt, providing some relief.

He was adding wood to the stove when he heard the stagecoach clatter into town. The

Fargo driver would stop to leave mail at the mercantile. Gabe walked to the window as soon as the potbelly was loaded, idly watching the stage driver carry a sack of letters to the door of Culpepper's, a larger bag than usual for a small town the size of Eagle Springs. It's nearly Christmas, he thought, an explanation for the bigger bag, people exchanging Christmas wishes. He thought about the need to cut down a small cedar tree so Martha could hang her decorations — strings of popcorn and small candles, the few colored glass balls they could afford. She would soon be making candy and cookies, and her delicious pecan pies, so sweet that the memory of them made his mouth water. He imagined what his wife would look like in a new yellow dress, with golden ribbons in her hair. Smiling unconsciously, he turned from the window to tackle a few papers he'd left undone earlier in the week.

But when he settled into his chair, his mind returned to the pair of killings, ten years apart. Something told him he'd been overlooking something obvious, a scrap of information he shouldn't have missed. Did it have to do with Johnny's death? Or the murder of Clarence Cummings? Nagged by the feeling, he put the sheets of foolscap aside to stare at the office wall.

* * *

A horse trotted up to the hitchrail. Outside the window, the sky darkened with the approach of nightfall and a covering of lead-gray storm clouds. Gabe had been working on a report for the county tax office, filling in a list of names from the delinquency rolls who would receive hand-delivered notices that action would be taken against them. Heavy boots clumped across the boardwalk and Gabe returned the pen to the inkwell.

A cowboy in a dirty mackinaw and a sweat-stained hat entered the office. Gabe recognized him at once. Will Jameson, the candidate he'd beaten for the sheriff's job, closed the door, then looked across the small room.

"Need a word with you, Sheriff," he said, his face sporting a week's worth of dark beard stubble. His attire hadn't been washed lately, judging by the scent that followed Jameson over to the stove. "I just found out Clarence Cummings was killed an' I may have seen the owlhoot who done it."

Gabe came out of his chair quickly, studying the cowboy's face. "Who did you see?"

"Never saw the feller before," Will said, frowning a little. "I was comin' across some of Cleve Wade's range, maybe a mile or two north of Beaver Draw. It was just about daylight, when I seen this tall gent, riding a big roan horse, headin' east like he was in one hell of a hurry. That was early yesterday mornin'. Struck me, why anybody would be runnin' a horse so hard, it bein' not quite sunup. I didn't think much more about it right then, until Peggy Wade told me that Clarence Cummings got hisself killed by a gunshot. The Cummings farm ain't far from where I seen that owlhoot runnin' his horse. So I come quick as I could, figurin' you'd want to know about the feller I seen, ridin' hard the other direction."

Gabe was stunned. "You say it was a big roan horse?" he asked, when he could find his voice.

"Yep," Will replied, nodding. "Kinda blue-colored, from a distance. The light wasn't all that good, bein' it was so early, but I'd call the horse a blue roan."

Gabe's next question had to be framed carefully. "Would you recognize the man if you saw him again?"

Will scowled as though it required some thought. "Most likely. I didn't get a good look at his face, but I figure I'd know him if I ever saw him again."

A flicker of doubt nudged Gabe's consciousness. "What were you doing out there at that early hour, riding cross-country?"

At that, the cowboy grinned. "I was headed

to the cookshack, lookin' fer a bite of breakfast. Cleve's been payin' me to ride night herd
lately, until his fall calves are old enough to
get clear of a pack of wolves. He's been havin'
a problem with wolf packs this fall. It don't
pay but ten a month and food, but I could
sure use the money. Cleve's real good about
takin' care of his friends during hard times."

"So I've found out," Gabe said, rubbing his
chin, thinking about Ramsey, now that there
was a witness to prove Ramsey was lying about
his whereabouts on the morning Clarence
died. "It's possible that the man you saw is
camped right here in Eagle Springs. I'd be
obliged if you'd come over to the creek with
me before you head back to the ranch. That
way, you can tell me if he's the same man
you saw riding away from the Cummings
farm."

Will nodded, glancing to the window. "It's
sure as hell liable to snow afore mornin'," he
said, then he gave Gabe a questioning look.
"You say there's a feller who looks like the
gent I saw, still hangin' around town?"

Gabe buttoned his coat and started for the
door. "That's the part that don't make sense,
but I'd be grateful if you looked him over.
If he's the right one, your testimony will be
enough for me to arrest him. A witness is what
I've been needing."

"I'll look," Will replied, following Gabe out of the office into a brisk wind hinting of moisture. "Can't say for sure that I'll recognize his face, but I'll damn sure know that horse if I ever see it again."

Gabe locked the door and led the way down Main Street, every now and then glancing up at the sky, watching for snowflakes, his mind on the moment when Will Jameson saw Ramsey and the blue roan gelding. Could it be a stroke of luck that the witness he needed showed up at just the right time? Maybe now, things would start to fall into place.

Another dark thought occurred to Gabe on the walk down to Justin Creek. If Will identified Ramsey as the man who galloped away from the scene of Clarence Cummings's murder, it would fall to Gabe to place the notorious gunman under arrest. Gabe easily recalled the promise Ramsey made, should Gabe ever try to take him with a gun.

Turning south off Main Street, Gabe's mouth went suddenly dry. He wondered if he would live to see what Martha looked like in her new yellow dress, live long enough to cut a small cedar tree for Christmas, enjoy her candy and cookies and pies.

CHAPTER 14

Ramsey was squatting on his haunches as Gabe and Will approached his camp fire. He palmed a tin cup of coffee, watching them warily, his attention drawn to Will Jameson more than to Gabe, if the direction of his stare could be judged. Twenty yards from Ramsey's tent, Will halted suddenly and aimed a finger at the live oak where the blue roan was tied.

"That's the same horse!" Will cried, then he looked at Ramsey. "And I reckon that's the same feller I saw ridin' away from the draw. Same hat, I'd nearly swear to it."

Gabe continued toward the fire, keeping an eye on Ramsey and the placement of his gun hand. He stopped when he was a few feet from the flames. For a time, there was an uneasy silence.

"I've got a witness here who says he saw you riding away from the Cummings farm early yesterday morning," Gabe began, aiming a thumb over his shoulder at Will. "If he's sure of the identification, then you lied to me."

Very slowly, Ramsey came to his feet. His eyes shifted from Gabe to Will. "Your witness is a liar," Ramsey said evenly, his right hand moving closer to the front of his coat.

Before Gabe could think about what was happening, Ramsey swept the tail of his canvas duster behind the butt of his holstered .44. He spread his feet slightly apart, crouching as though he meant to make a fast draw, the fingers on his right hand curled.

"Take it easy, Ramsey," Gabe protested, when he saw the gunman ready to go for his pistol. "All I'm doing is asking a few questions. This man is a local cowboy. He works at the Wade Ranch. He says he saw a man on a blue roan horse riding away from Beaver Draw yesterday, about daylight. Nobody else in these parts owns a roan like yours."

"I'd almost swear he's the same feller," Will said, lowering his voice some. "I'd stake my life that's the same blue horse."

Gabe opened his mouth to speak, then saw Ramsey claw his gun from its holster. Gabe's heart skipped a beat as he heard the hammer cocked.

"That's exactly what you're doin'," the gunman said, aiming at Will. "You've just staked your life on a lie. You never saw me or this roan horse yesterday."

"I'd damn near swear to it," Will replied,

much softer than before. "I reckon I could be wrong . . ."

"Put the gun away," Gabe warned with more courage than he felt right then. He had no doubt Ramsey would kill them both if things didn't go his way. Gabe knew it was too late to reach for his own pistol. It wasn't the sort of thing he would have tried in the first place against someone the likes of Buck Ramsey.

Ramsey gave him a look of quick irritation. "You must have me figured for a fool," he said. "I won't allow some cowpoke to ramrod me to the closest jail. Your witness is a damn liar, Sheriff. I don't care who he is, or what he claims he saw. I say he's a lyin' son of a bitch."

Gabe swallowed. At least Ramsey was willing to talk before he started shooting. "If you gun both of us down, there'll be warrants all over the state for your arrest. The Texas Rangers will have you before you've ridden fifty miles. If you're truly innocent of the shooting, you've got nothing to fear. Lower that gun. You'll have the chance to prove your case in court."

Ramsey almost smiled, just the beginnings, at the corners of his mouth. "What chance will I have?" he asked. "The deck is stacked against me. I believe I'll take my chances with the Rangers. That roan covers lots of ground. I won't let you put me in jail for a killing I didn't commit. You've got plenty more lookin' to do before you find out who shot that farmer. I didn't do it."

Gabe's palms were wet, despite the cold. This was the moment he'd been dreading, a direct confrontation with a professional gunfighter. He understood that his life hung in the balance, yet his pride wouldn't let him back down. "Then help me prove it. Surrender that gun and come with me peacefully. I can promise you a fair trial. I'll be working to find out the truth. If you didn't shoot Clarence Cummings, you've got nothing to worry about."

Now Ramsey was truly amused. A one-sided smile wrinkled his cheek. "If you had any sense, you'd see that somebody is tryin' to frame me. Some gent wants me out of the way, and I'd give long odds it's the same man who killed my brother."

"It's a possibility. But we're not getting any closer to the truth with that gun aimed at me. An innocent man would let the law handle it."

At that, Ramsey shook his head. "Not if the innocent man had to sit inside a jail cell, hoping a wet-nosed boy with a badge pinned to his chest could set him free. You're lettin' my brother's killer make a fool out of you, son. You're playin' right into his hands if you lock me away. I can't let you do it. Looks like I'll be forced to run afoul of the law to find out who shot Johnny." Ramsey swung his gun sights suddenly, aiming for Will's head. "Admit it's a goddamn lie, cowboy!" he snapped, tightening his finger around the trigger.

Will lifted his hands and took a step backward. "I don't want no trouble," he protested, a plea in his eyes when he looked at Gabe. "I ain't got a gun — don't let him shoot me, Sheriff. All I'm doin' is tellin' what I saw."

Despite the fact that Gabe had no real liking for Will Jameson, he stepped between Will and Ramsey's gun. "You can't threaten a witness like that," he warned. "Hand over the gun," he added, noticing that his knees felt weak, wondering if the next sound he heard would be the roar of a pistol. He extended his hand, watching Ramsey's trigger finger.

"Come any closer and I'll kill you," the gunman said with an unmistakable note of finality. He glanced in the direction of his horse. "I aim to pack up and clear out of this town. Send for the Rangers, if that's your inclination. I won't go to jail. Now back off, before I change my mind and shoot both of you. I won't be railroaded into another stretch in prison. I didn't kill that farmer. This so-called witness is a goddamn liar."

"You'll be making a mistake if you hightail it out of here," Gabe said. "You'll only be making things worse for yourself, so that it looks like you're guilty."

Ramsey turned his gun on Gabe, although his trigger finger relaxed a little. "I won't go to jail. Now back off, so I can load my gear without any bloodshed. If you've got good sense, you won't try to follow me. I've got nothin' against you, Sheriff. This ain't personal, but I'll have to kill you if you dog my trail. Remember, I warned you."

It was pointless to argue it further, so Gabe turned on his heel and spoke to Will. "Let's go. I've got a long ride ahead of me tonight, so I can wire the Texas Rangers from the Gatesville telegraph office."

Will needed no prodding to hurry away from Ramsey's gun. He walked beside Gabe in silence until they were close to Main Street. "He's the feller I saw that mornin'," Will said, glancing over his shoulder. "No doubt about it — he's the same one."

Gabe took a look at the creekbank before he spoke, catching a glimpse of Ramsey taking down his tent in the fading light. "I still can't figure why he would shoot Clarence. He came here to find his brother's killer. Anybody who knew Clarence will tell you he wasn't capable of murder, 'specially not a kid who was his son's best friend. So why would Ramsey kill him?"

When they reached Main, Will shrugged, looking briefly toward the saloon. "Believe I'll have myself a whiskey or two, after starin' down the barrel of that gun. I'll be down to fetch my horse later on." He turned to Gabe, with a glance down at Gabe's holstered pistol. "You damn near let that sidewinder take a shot at me," he complained. "How come you didn't draw that gun you're wearin'?"

Gabe didn't like the tone of the accusation. "Because I wanted to stay alive," he replied, not trying to hide the sarcasm in his voice.

Will regarded him with obvious disdain. "I told everybody you wouldn't make much of a lawman. If I'd won that election, I wouldn't let a hard case like Ramsey run his bluff on me."

The remark caused Gabe to square himself in front of Will, fighting to keep his temper under control. "You aren't much of a judge of men, if you thought Ramsey was bluffing just now. This town would have been having another election if you'd been wearing this star today. A funeral, and another election, if you'd been dumb enough to go for a gun against Buck Ramsey."

Gabe wheeled for the office, ducking down inside his coat to escape the wind, leaving Will standing in the middle of the road before he could reply to Gabe's prediction.

He explained the situation to Martha as he wolfed down his supper. "I've got to get off a wire to Ranger headquarters. I'll tell Sheriff Hunt what happened, but I figure we'll be too late to catch Ramsey in Coryell County. He'll be miles from here before sunrise. Looks like it's sure to snow, so a couple of Rangers should have an easy time following his tracks."

"You'll freeze on that mule's back tonight," Martha warned, bringing him his gloves, and a shawl for his head and ears. She stood beside his chair to watch him eat. "I'll bet you were surprised when Will Jameson showed up to tell you what he saw that morning," she added thoughtfully. "You were sounding like you were starting to believe Buck Ramsey when he told you he didn't go near the Cummings place the night before."

"More than surprised . . . ," he agreed, swallowing a last bit of biscuit, remembering Will's visit to the office. Gabe hadn't told his wife about the gun Ramsey aimed at them, not wanting to worry her.

He got up and pulled on his coat, taking the gloves and the wrap on his way to the

160

door. "It's liable to be after midnight before I get back," he said, bending down to kiss Martha's cheek. "I'll probably be frozen stiff, so leave that coffee on to warm."

He halted abruptly on the front porch when he saw a thin covering of snowflakes across the dark yard. Spits of snow drifted along on the wind, falling from a cloud-banked night sky. The mule and his saddle were dusted with tiny snowflakes. "This will be some miserable ride," he muttered, pulling his hat down tight to keep it from blowing off in the swirling winds. By the time he got to Gatesville he would be chilled to the bone, but the telegram had to be sent quickly if there was any hope the Rangers might corral Ramsey before he left the county.

He mounted the mule and shivered, reining the animal away from the porch to ride west through a building curtain of snowfall. Pulling on his gloves, he realized that his teeth had already begun to chatter before he had ridden a quarter of a mile.

Alone on the Gatesville road, every now and then he caught a glimpse of a lantern-lit window amid the snowflakes. He knew the names of most every family along the way, and sometimes, when he felt the coldest, he briefly considered riding up to one of the houses to warm himself at the fire. Each time, he resisted the urge and continued onward until he entered the sparsely populated ranch country where the road ran straight for several miles, past an old abandoned house surrounded by pecan trees. The house once belonged to a Confederate cavalry captain, Boyd Petrie, who was killed at Vicksburg. He'd called the place Pecan Grove, and the name stuck long after the house fell to ruin. Kids around Leon Junction claimed the old house was haunted, Gabe remembered. In daylight, the trees and a clear stream running through the grove made it a pretty place. Parts of Coryell County had dozens of deserted farmhouses because men like Captain Petrie didn't come back from the war.

Snow drifted across the road, accumulating where it fell away from the wind. Shivering inside his coat, teeth rattling, he came to a familiar bend and saw the outlines of pecan trees ahead, then the walls of the old house. "Sure be nice if those ghosts had a fire going in that fireplace," he mumbled, his lips gone numb from the cold. He sighted the crumbling chimney jutting above the roof as the mule carried him closer.

Just once, he thought he saw the faint glimmer of a fire through one of the windows. He told himself it was only his imagination, wishful thinking on a bitterly cold night. The house had been empty since the war and there were no such things as ghosts. Entering the trees where they lined the road, he almost missed a moving shadow crossing his path in the dark. The mule snorted and balked abruptly while Gabe was trying to see what frightened it. Then he saw the shadow clearly, the dark outline of a man blocking the road. The next sound he heard was the cocking of a gun.

CHAPTER 15

"Get down!" Gabe recognized the voice at once. "If you're still carryin' that gun, don't reach for it!"

Gabe tried to focus on Ramsey in the darkness; all he could see was a dim shape. The mule snorted again and bowed its neck. "I thought you'd be miles from here by now," Gabe said, still startled by Ramsey's sudden appearance as he took a boot from one stirrup to dismount. "You're not quite as clever as I figured."

As soon as Gabe reached the ground, Ramsey came over and stuck the gun against the front of his coat. "This has nothing to do with bein' smart," the gunman declared, lowering his voice, reaching inside Gabe's coat for his pistol. He jerked it roughly from its holster.

"Tie the mule out of the wind," Ramsey said, making a motion with his gun barrel. "You and me are gonna have a little talk. I've got a fire going in what's left of that old house."

Although Gabe was freezing, he said, "We've got nothing to talk about unless you're willing to give yourself up. You lied to me about where you were the morning Clarence Cummings was killed."

Ramsey leaned closer to Gabe's face, still holding the gun to Gabe's belly. "I told you the truth," he growled, his voice thick, angry.

Gabe led the mule off the road toward the house. His boots crunched through a few inches of accumulated snow, yet he barely heard the sound or thought about the badly needed moisture for next year's crops.

Ramsey trudged along behind him, and Gabe was sure the gun was still aimed at his back. Just then, the last thing Gabe would have considered was trying to make a break for it. Even if he could manage to get away, the gunman's horse would easily catch up to the much slower mule. Afoot, Gabe's chances looked no better, and now he was without his gun.

On the lee side of the old ruins, Gabe saw Ramsey's roan tied to a low limb of a pecan tree, away from most of the snowfall. Through a glassless window, he could see a fire flickering in the hearth. "It wasn't my imagination," he muttered to himself, securing the mule's reins to the tree with cold, trembling hands.

"Inside," Ramsey said, motioning with his gun barrel.

With Ramsey close at his heels, Gabe climbed rotted wooden steps at the front of the house, feeling the warmth of the fire as soon as he stepped into the front room. Above his head, where rafters had fallen away, a few snowflakes spiraled through holes in the roof, landing to form tiny piles across a sagging wood floor.

"How did you find this place?" Gabe asked, for the moment forgetting about the gun in Ramsey's hand.

Ramsey pointed to a pile of firewood close to the hearth where Gabe could sit near the flames. "You said you were headed to Gatesville to wire the Rangers. Wasn't all that hard to ride this road, lookin' for the likeliest spot to get the jump on you in the dark."

Gabe pulled off his gloves and held his hands above the fire, trying to steady them as welcome warmth slowly returned feeling to his fingers. "If you planned to kill me, why didn't you shoot me when I brought Jameson out to identify you?" Gabe looked over his shoulder, glancing down to the Colt in Ramsey's fist.

"I told you your witness is a damn liar!" Ramsey declared. "Whoever he's covering for is the man who killed my brother. Now who put him up to this?"

Gabe turned back to the fire. Outside, the

wind moaned around the eaves of the house, through the bare limbs of the nearby pecans. He thought about Ramsey's accusation. "I suppose it's possible. Will Jameson isn't exactly the most upstanding citizen we've got around Eagle Springs. Although he's been known to get mighty drunk on occasions, that doesn't make him an out-and-out liar. Still, he works for Cleveland Wade and my guess is he'd do whatever Wade told him."

"Tell me about this Wade." As Ramsey said it, he opened his duster and put away his pistol, though he still maintained a good distance from Gabe, watching him carefully in the firelight, his gun within easy reach.

"I hardly know him," Gabe began. "He came to Eagle Springs while the war was going on, bought up some of the best river bottomland with hard money, which was scarce back in those days. He runs cattle, mostly. I'd call him a boastful sort. He built a big, two-story house with a veranda across the front. He always rides the best horses money can buy."

Ramsey seemed to be pondering what Gabe said, remaining silent. In the firelight his pale eyes reflected the flames, making him look even more sinister. "Where did he come from?" Ramsey asked a moment later.

Gabe could only shrug. "I've got no idea. Never did hear him say. Me and him ain't all that friendly. He was backing someone else in our sheriff's election — the same Will Jameson who says he saw you out at the Cummings place that morning."

"What else do you know about Wade?"

"That's about it. For the most part, he pretty much has his way, on account of being so rich. He's real generous with some folks, mostly his neighbors, and the old widow woman we talked to about what happened to Johnny. Cleve gives her a little money now and then, for sugar and flour."

"Why would he do that?" Ramsey asked suspiciously.

"I reckon he feels sorry for her. That's what the man who owns the general store said. Harlan claimed it wasn't all that much, really."

Ramsey frowned. "Rich men are usually greedy," he said.

Gabe had no answer. He listened to the howl of the wind, waiting for Ramsey to reveal why he'd been waiting in the trees.

"I don't guess you would know this, but Ma was real pretty," he said softly, remembering. "After Pa died, men used to stare at her. She moved us up here to get away from all the sad memories, she told us. But I always figured it was for other reasons too, like the way men looked at her. She liked small towns. She took to Eagle Springs the minute she saw

it. Then the conscription order was posted an'
I had to leave before we hardly got settled.
Ma and Johnny were real happy here when
I left . . ."

Gabe heard the terrible sorrow in Ramsey's
voice. "It must have been hard, to learn about
what happened to them."

Ramsey's face changed, his cheeks frozen.
"I've waited a long time to settle the score
with the bastard who killed my brother. I
won't let anybody stand in my way. I didn't
kill that farmer — he was scared when I questioned him about Ma's wagon. He knew something, and I intended to find out what it was.
Somebody killed him before I got the
chance. I think he knew where my ma went,
only he was afraid to say. I'm guessin' he was
tryin' to protect somebody he knew real well.
The farmer was damn sure alive the last time
I saw him."

Gabe thought about it a moment. Standing
so close to the fire, he'd stopped shivering.
"If you're telling the truth, it makes Will
Jameson a liar."

"I never saw the man before," Ramsey
stated flatly. "You've got to decide whether
you believe me, or him. Somebody told him
what I looked like, what color horse I ride,
that I questioned that farmer the day before.
Somebody told him what to say."

169

Gabe remembered the talk with Cleve in front of the office. "I suppose that could have been Cleveland Wade. He drove all the way to town, demanding to know why I hadn't arrested you for killing Clarence. He said he aimed to drive over to Gatesville to complain to the county judge that I wasn't moving fast enough. Will showed up later that same afternoon, to tell me about seeing you out at Beaver Draw. Some coincidence —"

"Or a frame-up," Ramsey said.

Gabe sighed, wondering who was telling the truth. He would be taking a stand against one of the county's leading citizens if he believed Ramsey's version. Staring vacantly at a wall, he barely noticed a handful of snowflakes that floated down from a gaping hole in the roof. "I'm caught between a rock and a hard place," he said. "To tell you the honest truth, I don't know who to believe. Everything about your story fits the circumstances. On the other hand, I've got a witness who puts you at the scene of a murder. I saw you out there myself, the day before Clarence got shot. You admit to questioning Clarence about your ma's disappearance. Tell me straight — did you ask those questions with a gun in your hand?"

"No. I swear it."

"I've only got your word that you didn't

kill him," Gabe answered. "Why should I believe you?"

"The only reason I'd kill the farmer is if I had found out he was the one who killed my brother. In that case, I would've left town, because the only reason I'm here is to find out who shot Johnny and what happened to Ma. The fact that I'm still here should tell you I'm not the one who's lying."

Gabe considered the logic carefully. "If I believe your story, it makes Will Jameson an out-and-out liar, and most likely points a finger at Cleveland Wade. But we still don't have a motive for Cleve killing Johnny, or any evidence of what happened to your ma."

"Just one more question," Ramsey said, coming a step closer to Gabe, lowering his voice so he was hard to hear. "Tell me about Wade's wife."

"He doesn't have one. Somebody told me his wife died giving birth to their daughter, Peggy Sue, nineteen or twenty years ago."

A fire of another kind burned behind Ramsey's eyes just then, having nothing to do with the flames in the fireplace. He merely nodded and inclined his head toward the opening where the front door stood ajar. "You're free to go," he said quietly. "I think you've told me all I need to know." He took Gabe's gun from the waistband of his denims, opened the loading gate, and rodded all six cartridges onto the floor. The shells clattered around his boots, then he handed the empty gun over to Gabe. "I hope you won't send that wire to the Texas Rangers just yet," he continued. "I think I know who killed Johnny, and I expect Ma's dead too. All I'm gonna find is her bones."

Gabe fisted the gun. "You think Cleve took her, don't you," he said. "You think he killed both of them . . ."

Ramsey didn't answer him. He turned his back on Gabe and walked across the floor, rattling his big spur rowels on the boards. He went around the doorframe and vanished into the darkness. Gabe listened to the sound of his spurs on the porch, then the softer crunch of boots through the snow. A minute later, he heard the roan trot away from the house.

Gabe remained by the fire, staring at the flames, planning his next move very carefully with a certain amount of disbelief. He had always prided himself for taking a cautious approach in important matters. So why was he even considering doing anything else, when his and Martha's future could be at stake?

CHAPTER 16

Martha heard him come in, even though the hour was late. She came to the kitchen, wrapped in her robe, while he greedily drank hot coffee beside the warmth of the cookstove.

"I didn't send that wire," he said, still shivering from the long ride back through the wind and snow. "Buck Ramsey was waiting for me at the old Petrie farm. He ordered me out of the saddle at gunpoint so we could talk."

Martha was clearly puzzled. "Why didn't you send for the Rangers?"

Gabe thought about his decision. "Because some of what Ramsey said makes sense. I don't think he killed Clarence Cummings. I think Will Jameson was sent to town to put the blame on Ramsey. I believe Will was lying about the whole thing."

"Who would put him up to it?" Martha asked.

He poured another cup of coffee, remembering what was said at the old house. "Ramsey thinks it's Cleve Wade's doing. Clarence must have known Cleve killed Johnny."

"It sounds pretty farfetched," Martha said, watching her husband's face turn ruddy from the stove's heat. "You'll have a hard time getting anyone around here to believe that Cleve Wade is behind any of this."

"He has lots of friends," Gabe agreed. "I'll have plenty of enemies in this town if I've gambled wrong. But there's a ring of truth to what Ramsey says. For the time being, I'm going to trust him while I poke around out at the Wade ranch. Ramsey also implied that Cleve may have had something to do with the disappearance of his mother. Ramsey asked me a strange question, just before he rode away from Pecan Grove. He wanted to know about Cleve's wife. When I told him that Cleve's wife died giving birth to Peggy Sue, he didn't act surprised. He almost acted like he expected to hear it. He made another remark too, something about finding his ma's bones. I wonder if he expects to find them out at the Wade ranch . . . ?"

"This isn't like you, Gabe," Martha insisted, "to believe in some fanciful story about how one of the town's most respected citizens could be the murderer of a defenseless boy. Who else is going to believe a story like that?"

"Hardly anybody, I'm afraid. Unless I can get my hands on some proof." Then some-

174

thing Martha said made him pause. "You called Johnny Ramsey defenseless just now, only he wasn't. Harvey said something about finding an old shotgun next to the body. Maybe that's the angle I'm missing. Why would a boy Johnny's age be carrying a shotgun?"

"Maybe he was hunting coons that night," Martha said.

"Or he felt threatened by something happening at his house," Gabe said. "Maybe he saw something . . . someone . . . who he believed meant to harm his mother. He might have been expecting someone like that and waited down at the creek for whoever it was to show up."

"Then why didn't Miz Hawkins hear some sort of disturbance that night?" Martha asked.

"I think she did," Gabe replied softly. "That's why she got so upset when I kept pressing her about it."

"It's all speculation," Martha reminded him. "You don't have a shred of proof."

"I know," he whispered, staring blankly out the kitchen window at the snowflakes.

A blanket of snow covered the hills and shallow valleys around Eagle Springs, and more continued to fall as Gabe rode to town an hour past dawn. Otherwise occupied, he hardly noticed the animal tracks in the snow, where rabbits and other small game ventured across the road, or the much larger prints of wandering deer. He kept remembering the talk with Buck Ramsey and the dark conclusions they had drawn. If Cleve had wanted Anna Ramsey back then, he'd have come courting, perhaps in his shiny black carriage. Why would he abduct her or attack her in any way?

As Gabe rode across the ridge above Eagle Springs, he wondered where Ramsey was hiding now. Gabe was sure the gunman had watched him leave the Petrie house and knew from the direction he rode that he hadn't wired for the Rangers. Was he someplace close to the Wade ranch this morning, nosing around for clues to Anna's disappearance? Gabe would hear plenty about it if anyone saw Ramsey near Cleve's property. Cleve himself would be the loudest to complain. A thing like that would get the whole town up in arms and the blame would fall on Gabe for failing to put Ramsey in jail.

He rode down Main Street, noting that hardly anyone was out and about in the snowstorm. It seldom ever snowed in Coryell County. Had it not been for more pressing matters, Gabe would have enjoyed the beauty of it.

Before he reached the office, he spotted Roy

Culpepper shoveling snow from the porch of the mercantile. The store's windows looked warm and inviting, aglow with lantern light, sporting Christmas decorations. The Christmas ornaments reminded Gabe of the yellow cloth he needed to buy for Martha, the ribbon, and the bottle of rose scent. Instead of stopping at the office, Gabe headed for the store to make his purchases, Christmas being so close, just three days away.

"Mornin', Roy," he said, halting the mule near the steps. "I need to buy a few Christmas gifts for my wife, soon as you're done shoveling."

Roy leaned on the handle of his shovel. "I was lookin' for an excuse to quit," he said. "Been meanin' to ask you, Gabriel, what come of that no-account gunslick?"

Gabe swung down. He knew he should expect a lot of questions like Roy's. "He cleared out yesterday evening. Can't say where he went."

"How come you didn't arrest him for killing Clarence Cummings?" Roy's tone wasn't friendly when he asked.

"I can't prove he did it just yet, but I'm working on it," Gabe explained.

The scowl on the storekeeper's face deepened.

"You know damn good an' well he did it,"

Roy said. "We ain't had a killing round here in a coon's age. Buck Ramsey shows up and right away, a good citizen of this town is dead. How much more proof do you need? Will Jameson swears he saw Ramsey leavin' the Cummings farm early that same mornin'. Looks to me like that oughta be enough to convince you."

Gabe was about to tie the mule to the hitchrail, but when he heard the tone of Roy's remarks, he decided against it. "There was no witness to the shooting," he told him.

"Nearly the same thing, what Will saw," Roy argued. He paused to take a breath. "Some of us got together last night down at the Broken Spoke to talk things over. Will told us how you backed down from Ramsey. There's some around here who think maybe you ain't up to doin' your job, Gabriel. Will said you flat-out tucked your tail between your legs in front of Ramsey, like you was scared plumb to death of him."

Gabe was more surprised than ever, hearing Roy accuse him of cowardice. The two of them had always gotten along. "He held a gun on me," Gabe protested. "Did Will bother to mention that?"

"Don't remember exactly," Roy muttered. "He said you acted scared."

"Harvey warned me that Buck Ramsey is

178

a dangerous man. I'm not looking to get myself killed. I aim to put out a wire to the Texas Rangers on him, just as soon as I've got some proof that'll stand up in court."

Roy wagged his head. "I'm real disappointed in you, Gabriel, and there's some other folks in this town who feel the same. I know you're a touch on the young side, but you hadn't oughta try to hold down a man's job if you ain't able to do it."

Roy's last remark stung Gabe deeply. "Sorry you and the others feel that way," he said quietly. "I've always tried to do my best." He looked up at the leaden sky briefly, feeling snowflakes brush his cheeks. "I believe I'll wait to buy those gifts for Martha. It's still snowing and I've got some things I need to look into."

Roy lifted his shovel again. "You probably figure we're bein' too hard on you," he said, eyeing more snow on the steps. "We expected you to take some sort of action when a good man like Clarence gets gunned down in his own barn. By the way, his burial is this afternoon. Carl already got the hole dug."

"I'll be there," Gabe replied, climbing back in the saddle, knowing his face had turned red. "Maybe by then I'll be able to prove who killed him."

Before Gabe could ride off, Roy gave him

a chilly stare. "Hell, everybody 'cept you already knows who done it. Can't figure why you're bein' so hardheaded about it. Last night, Cleve Wade said this proves we voted the wrong man for sheriff. I sure do hope it turns out he's wrong about you."

He was playing a hunch, stopping off at Harvey's house. With what the townspeople were saying about him, it seemed he had little to lose. Climbing the front steps, Gabe was still red-faced over the things Roy said. He knocked on Harvey's door, trying to push Roy's words from his mind.

The door opened and Bernice looked out. She smiled and said, "Do come in, Gabriel. Isn't it lovely that we're having a white Christmas? Harvey's been watching it snow from the bedroom window."

"Yes, ma'am, it sure is pretty," he answered, pulling off his hat. "You reckon Harvey feels well enough to talk to me for a minute?"

"Of course he does," she said, beckoning him toward the bedroom. "He thinks so much of you, Gabriel, almost like you were a son to him."

She showed him into the room. Harvey turned his head on the pillow and grinned weakly, the bloody cup towel clamped in one hand.

"Mornin', Gabe," he said. "And a merry Christmas to you an' Martha. Makes it special, when it snows on Christmas."

Gabe walked over to the bed. Harvey's color was worse than before. "I needed to ask a few things, if you feel up to it."

Harvey's expression turned serious. "It has to do with that Buck Ramsey, don't it?"

Gabe nodded. "I'm afraid so. Roy just told me half the town has turned against me because I haven't arrested Ramsey for the murder of Clarence Cummings. I can't prove Ramsey did it. I've questioned him about it, and his answers seem to fit."

"He's a well-known troublemaker," Harvey said, sighing. "You should expect folks to put the blame on him. Eagle Springs is a quiet town. This sort of thing never happens here."

"I know," Gabe said, glancing out the window for a moment. "Ramsey has other ideas about what happened. At first, it sounded pretty farfetched. The trouble is, some of it makes sense. If you'll listen, I'd like to tell you what Ramsey has to say."

Harvey's gaze drifted to the ceiling above his bed. He swallowed once. "I'll listen," he said softly. "Pull up that chair over yonder. I've got a feelin' this is gonna take a spell."

Gabe carried a straight-backed wooden chair to the bed and eased his weight into it.

181

"Some of this will sound a little crazy at the beginning," he said. "When Ramsey told me who he thinks is behind all of this, I thought he'd gone loco. But when you add it all up, it's about the only way to explain what happened to his brother ten years ago, and why Miz Ramsey disappeared the way she did. It still don't provide all the answers, the reasons why it could have happened the way Ramsey claims. But if he's right, I know why Clarence was shot. And it means I've got one heck of a big problem on my hands, deciding what's to be done to prove it one way or the other."

Harvey turned his face to the window. "Tell me about it," he whispered. "Tell me what Buck had to say. Maybe you oughta get up an' close that bedroom door. I wouldn't want to worry Bernice, bein' it's so close to Christmas."

Gabe went to the door and closed it gently, wondering if perhaps now someone who knew what really happened to the Ramsey boy and his mother was willing to talk about it. Or was Harvey simply curious to find out how much Gabe had learned on his own?

CHAPTER 17

Harvey didn't say a word the entire time Gabe laid out the details of his meeting with Buck Ramsey. After Gabe finished, Harvey silently stared at a nearby window. Then he looked at Gabe and asked in a phlegmy voice, "You think I know, don't you? You think I'm keepin' something from you . . ."

"I've wondered about it from time to time. I got the feeling Miz Hawkins knows more than she's willing to tell, and every now and then, I wonder if you've told me everything you found out back then."

A violent cough shook the old man's chest. Pain brought traces of tears to his eyes as he wiped bloody spittle from his lips. He caught his breath, then let out a whispering sigh. "I don't know anything for sure," he said in a voice so quiet Gabe had to lean closer to the bed to hear him. "Buck's right about one thing — Clara knows what happened that night. She's too terrified to tell anyone about it. Right off, I suspected Cleve Wade was the man she's afraid of, but there was no way to prove a damn thing." He watched Gabe's face closely now. "Always was proud of my record as sheriff of this town, if I didn't count the fact that I never could figure out what happened that night, or who was to blame. I done the best I could. I've had my suspicions about Cleve all along. I reckon I oughta tell you why."

Gabe waited, moving to the edge of his chair.

"Cleve took a fancy to Anna Ramsey right from the start," Harvey began, speaking just above a whisper. "He'd come by her house, all decked out in his best ridin' gear, makin' a show of inquiring about her welfare, hers and the boy's, bein' they was all alone after Buck went to war. He'd stop off at Clara's place too, makin' the same inquiry. Hardly anybody thought much about it. Folks used to talk about how thoughtful he was, makin' sure two of the town's widows had enough to eat while that war was going on. Preacher Sims told the congregation one Sunday mornin' what a fine man he thought Cleve was, seein' after helpless widows like that. It got to where hardly anybody noticed when Cleve rode down to the creek."

When Harvey paused, Gabe asked, "What made you suspicious of him?"

The old man cleared his throat and mopped

his mouth with the towel. "I talked to the boy about it one time, how he oughta be glad Cleve dropped by to see to their needs when times were so hard for nearly everybody. That's when I knew somethin' was wrong. Johnny sorta bristled over Cleve's visits, sayin' how he wished that rich feller would leave his ma alone. He said his ma told Cleve not to come around no more, only he did anyways. The boy acted mighty concerned. Wasn't long after that, we found Johnny dead and Miz Ramsey gone."

Gabe nodded when Harvey paused again. "Did you question Cleve after it happened?"

Harvey closed his eyes briefly. "I did. I suppose you could say I tried. I rode out to the ranch after I lost those wagon tracks. Cleve came out on the porch when I rode up, like he damn near expected to see me. When I asked him if he knew about what happened to the boy, and that Miz Ramsey had turned up missing, he went on about how terrible it was. Sounded downright grieved about it. He offered to do anything he could to help find out who'd done such an awful thing. Said he was glad his daughter was off at boarding school, what with some killer on the loose."

Harvey's voice had grown weaker, forcing Gabe to listen carefully to each word. "What was it that aroused your suspicions?" he asked.

"I can't see much wrong with his offering to help find out who did it."

"Wasn't that," Harvey whispered. "I asked him if he'd seen Miz Ramsey's wagon pass that way. Told him I'd followed her tracks to Beaver Draw an' lost 'em in the rocks. He said he never saw no wagon. Found out later, he'd have to have been blind not to have seen it."

Suddenly, a series of coughing spasms shook the old man's chest, and for a time he held the towel in front of his mouth and tried to clear his lungs. A moment later, Bernice tapped lightly on the bedroom door, then entered the room hurriedly and rushed to her husband's bedside.

"That'll have to be all for today, Gabriel," she said, worry in her eyes as she helped Harvey wipe the blood from his lips. "He simply must rest now."

Gabe stood up and said, "Yes, ma'am," desperately wishing there could have been time to ask Harvey what he meant about the wagon. He backed to the door slowly and showed himself out while Bernice was ministering to her dying husband. Out on the porch, he found some satisfaction in the discovery that most of what Harvey told him fit the circumstances Buck Ramsey described. More and more, things pointed to Cleve Wade.

The place to start looking for more clues was at the Wade ranch. Gabe understood that things were already set to explode between him and Cleve. Poking around out there, asking questions, was sure to bring the pot to a boil.

He mounted the mule and looked north, the direction of the Wade ranch. It would require nerves of steel to ride to Cleve's doorstep, now that the rancher had his back up over Gabe's refusal to arrest Ramsey the day before. It was likely that Cleve would try to order him off the place before the first question was asked. But with no place else to begin proving Cleve's guilt or innocence, Gabe wheeled the mule north and drummed his heels against the animal's sides, still wondering what Harvey meant when he talked about Anna Ramsey's wagon.

The house sat on a hilltop overlooking broad expanses of unfenced land. Beneath a mantle of snow, the rolling hills and shallow valleys made a pretty sight. Here and there, groups of fat longhorn cattle stood with their tails to the wind, their backs dusted with snowflakes as they pawed through the snow to graze. Gabe rode toward the imposing two-story house with misgivings. The last thing he wanted was to touch off an angry confrontation with Cleve just now, not until he had some sort of solid proof of the rancher's involvement. It was one thing to speculate over what might have happened that night ten years ago, but to prove it would be an entirely different matter. What possible evidence could there be so many years later? Again, Gabe wished Harvey could have told him what he meant about the wagon.

A winding lane took him to the house. A black dog began barking, announcing his arrival. Behind the house, barns and corrals made an impressive display of the size of the cattle operation Cleve owned. A tiny bunkhouse sat near the pole corrals where a few saddle horses grazed on a mound of snow-covered hay. Fifty yards from the front porch surrounding three sides of the main house, Gabe slowed the mule to a walk when he saw someone come outside. He waved a friendly greeting, feeling some relief from the worry burdening him on the ride from Eagle Springs. Peggy Sue, clad in her sheepskin coat, walked to the edge of the porch, smiling back at him as she turned up her coat collar to keep out wind-driven snowflakes.

"How are you, Gabriel?" she asked when he brought the mule to a halt near the porch steps. "What brings you out in this terrible weather?"

He waited to dismount, wondering if he'd be welcome when he announced his purpose. "I wanted to talk to Cleve a minute, if he ain't busy."

The young woman cast a look to the west. "I'm afraid he's not here just now, and I'm a little worried. He rode over to Gatesville on his favorite thoroughbred colt. That two-year-old is still green-broke. I sure hope nothing has happened . . ."

"I've heard it said that your pa's a fine horseman, Peggy Sue. Maybe he's traveling slow on account of the snow."

"I hope you're right," she said, still sounding worried. Then she looked at Gabe again. "It's because of you that he went, you know," she added darkly. "He's mad as a nest of hornets because you didn't put Buck Ramsey in jail. He wanted to talk to Judge Green and Sheriff Hunt, to complain that you didn't arrest Ramsey when you had the chance."

"I tried to tell your pa what I was up against, that I needed solid proof before I can bring charges against Ramsey, but he hardly listened to a word I said."

A gust of cold wind swept more snow across the porch, causing the girl to shiver. "Pa's like that sometimes. He can have an awful temper. He blames it on our Irish blood," she added with a smile. "He claims I've got a temper, too. Why don't you climb down and come inside so you can warm yourself by the fire. I'm sure Pa wouldn't mind."

Gabe glanced over his shoulder. "I shouldn't," he told her, despite the fact that he was freezing. "My folks taught me that it wasn't proper for a married man to be alone in the same house with a single woman. People might talk, and I wouldn't want your pa to have any more reason to be mad at me. But I'm obliged for the offer anyway. I can't remember ever being so cold."

Something he said made her giggle. "Don't be silly, Gabriel. Come inside and get warm. Not meaning any disrespect toward your parents, but that's an old-fashioned notion about married men and what's proper."

Her invitation proved too tempting. "Maybe just for a minute or two," he said, swinging a leg over the mule's rump to dismount. He tied the reins to a porch post and climbed the steps on numbed legs to follow her into the house.

The front room was the largest Gabe had ever seen, with a huge fireplace in the far wall giving off wonderful heat. Peggy Sue motioned him over to the fire, across a polished wooden floor, past expensive upholstered chairs and a loveseat flanked by delicate wood tables with carved legs. Oil paintings hung on the walls. Everything he saw befit the home of a wealthy man. He wiped the snow off his boots on a small piece of rug near the door and went to the fireplace.

Once again, the girl seemed amused by something he'd done.

"You're very polite, aren't you?" she asked.

He could only shrug and grin back at her. "Not so's anybody ever noticed before," he answered, feeling some embarrassment when he looked at her too long, thinking how pretty she was, almost as pretty as Martha. To put his mind on other things he opened the front of his coat to allow some of the warmth in. It was then that the girl saw he was wearing a gun and the smile left her face.

"You don't usually carry a pistol," she said. "Is it because of that gunfighter being here?"

"More or less," he admitted, looking away, wondering if Cleve told his daughter about Gabe backing down from Ramsey. "I haven't found a need for it yet. I can't prove a thing against Buck Ramsey."

"Why did you want to talk to my pa about it?" she asked, her tone anything but friendly now.

He debated how far he should go with Peggy Sue, how much to tell her about his suspicions. "There are some things that don't stack up about the killing of Johnny Ramsey and the disappearance of Anna, the boy's mother. Cleve was here back then. I wanted to ask him a few questions, to see what he remembered. Harvey Barnes told me that your pa was real taken with Anna when she first came to Eagle Springs. Cleve used to drop by her house now and then, Harvey said. Harvey said Miz Ramsey was a real pretty lady."

At that, the girl scowled. "Do you think my pa had anything to do with her disappearance?" There was an unmistakable edge to her voice.

He understood that it could only make matters worse to accuse Cleve in front of his daughter until there was some proof that the rancher knew more than he'd been willing to tell Harvey back then. "I'd have no reason to think anything like that," he replied. "I only wondered if he had any idea where the woman might have gone after her son died. If your pa knew her better than most folks, maybe he's got some notion of where she went, or why she didn't tell anybody she was leaving."

For a moment, the girl looked past him to a window, as though trying to remember something. "I was away at boarding school in Fort Worth when it happened," she said. "I hated that place, but Pa sent me so I wouldn't be left alone while he was out tending cattle. Pa knew I loved this ranch. After I wrote him enough letters, begging him to let me come home, he drove up and got me. But that was a year or so after Johnny was killed. I don't recall that Pa talked about it all that much.

"I don't think he ever really got over it when my ma died. Last spring, while I was doing the spring cleaning, I found some of Ma's old dresses up in the attic. I never knew him to be sentimental. I was surprised when I found those clothes. He kept them almost twenty years, and that isn't like him at all, to keep things around when they aren't useful."

Gabe hadn't been listening all that closely at first, paying more attention to Peggy Sue's beautiful face and the soft sound of her voice. But when she mentioned finding a woman's dresses in the attic, an idea entered his thoughts. Could the dresses have belonged to Anna Ramsey? Hadn't Harvey said that one of the most difficult things to explain about Anna's sudden disappearance was the fact that she'd taken all her clothes from the shack down by the creek, making it look like she left of her own free will? It was one reason why Gabe never believed Harvey's suggestion about the drifter.

A cold chill ran down Gabe's back. He

glanced up at the ceiling, thinking about the attic. There might be proof up there that Cleveland Wade brought Anna Ramsey to this very house after the murder of her son.

He looked at the flames to avoid any chance of revealing what he was thinking just then. Peggy Sue wouldn't know anything about it, being away at school at the time. It was just a guess . . .

Gabe turned to a front window, watching the snowfall. He was having trouble making himself believe that Anna Ramsey's remains might be lying out there somewhere underneath a few inches of snow.

CHAPTER 18

The sound of Peggy Sue's voice startled him.

"You must be thinking some real deep thoughts," she said, smiling when he turned quickly from the window.

"Sorry," he muttered, certain that a flush was creeping into his cheeks. "You said something about finding some of your ma's clothes in the attic. I suppose that's what I was thinking about, why Cleve kept them so many years. Seems like he'd have gotten rid of them. I didn't mean to be rude, staring out that window so long. Lately, my mind's been on the Johnny Ramsey killing, now that Buck has shown up asking questions about it. Sometimes I sort of drift off, wondering who could have killed the boy, and what happened to Miz Ramsey. Harvey said the woman drove off in her wagon. He followed the wagon tracks to Beaver Draw, and that's where he lost them. Harvey mentioned something about that wagon when I talked to him this morning, only he was too sick to finish what he wanted to say. It got me to thinking that maybe, if I could find out what happened to the wagon, I'd be closer to knowing why Miz Ramsey disappeared. It sounds downright impossible, to track down a wagon ten years later. But I got the feeling that's what Harvey wanted me to do . . . unless he already knows what came of the wagon. Maybe he'll be strong enough tomorrow to tell me what was on his mind."

Peggy Sue gave him an understanding nod. "He didn't give you much to go on, sounds like," she agreed. "How could you expect to find a wagon that's been missing for ten years? Besides not knowing where it went, or what it looked like, since you're almost as young as me and you'd hardly be expected to re-member something like that when you were nine or ten."

"I wasn't living here then," he confessed. "I grew up over at Leon Junction, so I never knew any of the Ramseys, or what kind of wagon they owned. I got the feeling that Har-vey was aiming to tell me where to look for it, maybe, like he already knew where it was, or which way it went when Anna Ramsey left the county."

Now the girl shook her head. "This county's full of old abandoned farms with tumbledown wagons. Pa said when the war was over, a whole bunch of farmers didn't come back and the families had to move on. How will you know it's the right wagon if you find it?"

He could only shrug. "I'm hoping Harvey can tell me what to look for, soon as he's feeling better. Maybe there's something unusual about the Ramseys' wagon that'll tell me if I find the right one."

Peggy Sue looked like she was remembering something. "A few years back I rode up on what was left of a wagon down by the Leon, while I was looking for strays. Somebody had burned it. It was just a pile of ashes. Hardly anything left but the iron wheel rims. I could tell it happened a long time ago — weeds had grown so thick around it you could hardly tell it was there, or what it was."

He cleared his throat. "Whereabouts along the river did you find it?" he asked, trying to sound only mildly interested.

She appeared to have no trouble recalling it. "Where our ranch joins the old Neff place, right above the falls. Hardly anybody ever goes there. Like I told you, I was checkin' for strays when —" The girl stopped abruptly. The look she gave Gabe would have melted ice. "Tell me why you want to know. Are you implying that Miz Ramsey's wagon could have been burned on this ranch and that my pa could have had something to do with it?"

He shook his head quickly. "I wasn't saying that at all, Peggy Sue. Honest. I was just wondering about it."

Still somewhat doubtful, she agreed with a silent movement of her head.

"I'd better be going," he said, making a half turn away from the fireplace. "I'm grateful for you allowing me in so I could melt the icicles off my nose. My mule's liable to be froze so stiff he can't make it back to town. Much obliged for your hospitality, and please give my best to your pa when he gets back. I'll ride out to see him some other time when the weather's more favorable."

He walked to the door and donned his hat, then let himself out into the falling snow. While he was boarding the mule, he risked a glance up at the roof of the house, hoping Peggy Sue wouldn't notice that he was looking at the attic space. Pulling the mule around, he couldn't help but wonder if the attic contained the secret to Anna Ramsey's disappearance, perhaps hidden inside an old trunk. But as the mule trotted away into a stiff crosswind, Gabe knew it would be next to impossible to prove that a trunkful of dresses belonged to the missing woman. Unless there was something else hidden with the clothing that would clearly identify its owner.

When he was more than a mile from the

house, out of sight from the front porch in a stand of live oaks, he halted the mule to gaze eastward, to where the dark line of the Leon River followed a broad valley angling south. Barren cottonwoods, limbs heavy with accumulated snow, drooped above the river, marking its passage. Gabe knew the spot where the Wade ranch joined the Neff property, though he'd been there only once or twice, to try a little fishing below the falls. The layer of snow would make the burned-out wagon that much harder to find. Resting in the saddle with his back to the wind, he wondered what a pile of ashes and charred wheel rims stood to prove. The only thing about the discovery of a burned wagon on Wade property was that it tended to support Buck Ramsey's notion that Cleve had something to do with his mother's disappearance.

"It wouldn't be enough to convince Judge Green," Gabe said aloud, his teeth starting to chatter again. "But I suppose it's worth a try, just to see if I can find it."

He reined the mule toward a shallow ravine that would take him down to the river without being seen from the house. The ride would take several hours and he would miss lunch with Martha, but when he told her about the day's events, particularly Peggy Sue's revelations about the dresses in the attic and the burned wagon, Gabe knew she would understand. Tomorrow was Sunday. He could explain his ideas to her on the drive to church, if he got back too late tonight. A special Christmas service was planned by Reverend Sims that would bring everyone from this end of the county. He found himself wishing again that he could have afforded to buy his wife a ready-made dress for the occasion this year.

Riding into the curtain of snowflakes, he wondered what he would find above the Leon River falls. He pondered, too, what it would prove if he found the remains of a wagon. He would be laughed right out of the office of sheriff if he tried to convince anyone that a pile of ashes made Cleveland Wade a killer. His best chance of proving anything against Cleve might be in the attic, but he concluded that he would have to be completely mad to risk finding out for himself. Cleve would most certainly kill him if he found him up there, if the attic contained the personal belongings of Anna Ramsey.

His arms and legs were numb. There was no feeling in his hands and fingers. Trudging through deep snowdrifts, he had crossed back and forth along the riverbank at the top of the falls, pawing through stands of thick brush, to find nothing. The snow prevented him from seeing much of anything on the ground. Panting, his breath coming from his lips in frosty curls, he straightened near a cutbank and shook his head. "The snow's too damn deep," he mumbled, shivering, casting what he meant to be a final glance up and down the river. He'd been looking for hours, losing all track of time. The snowfall had lessened some, though the sky was still a dull gray, preventing him from guessing the hour by the slant of the sun.

His gaze roamed here and there, until his frozen feet started to ache from the cold. The walk back to the cottonwood tree where he tied the mule would take him through some of the deepest drifts, so he decided to climb to the top of the bank where the going would be easier. Starting forward, his head bent to the ground, his eyes landed on a curious circle in the snow near a pile of thorny vines. The vines had shed their leaves for winter, making the odd round spot easy to see. Gabe shoved his freezing hands into his coat pockets and plodded over to the thicket, where he nudged the edge of the circle with the toe of his boot.

He leaned down quickly when he heard the dull ring of iron. Working his fingers into the snowflakes, he seized a flat metal object and pulled it off the ground.

"It's a wheel rim!" he exclaimed, no longer

aware of the cold. He noted the iron rim's charred appearance. Unconsciously, he smiled. "It was burned," he said, much softer now. He stared at the heavy object a while longer, wondering if it could possibly be a part of Anna Ramsey's wagon.

He took his bearings, so he would remember the place. He dropped the rim back in the snow and dusted off his hands. A little voice inside his head told him that finding the rim was an important discovery. Now all he had to do was find a way to prove that one of the county's most influential citizens had been responsible for burning a critical piece of evidence, evidence that would mark him as a murderer if anyone put all the missing pieces of the puzzle together.

Gabe climbed the riverbank slowly, knowing what had to be done next. Somehow, he had to see what was hidden away in Cleve Wade's attic. Trudging toward his mule, he knew it would be the most dangerous undertaking of his lifetime, even more dangerous than facing a killer like Buck Ramsey that time on the banks of Justin Creek.

A lone horseman approached from the southwest. The chestnut trotted easily along the wagon ruts. Gabe spotted the rider a quarter mile away, puzzling over who else might be out on a day like this during a snowstorm. He'd been preoccupied with his findings on the banks of the Leon, sorting through possibilities, until he noticed the distant traveler. At first, before he could make out the color of the horse the man was riding, he had worried that it might be Buck Ramsey. But when a closer look revealed the chestnut's coat, he relaxed a little. Then his fears returned when he recognized the rider's bulk. He was headed straight for an encounter with Cleve Wade, and just then, it was the last thing he wanted.

Gabe stopped the mule in the middle of the road when Cleve was only a few yards away. The rancher's broad face showed no friendliness when he sighted Gabe. Cleve hauled back on the chestnut's reins, then stared at Gabe for a time, his lips drawn into a thin line.

"I've been over to the county seat to talk to Judge Green," Cleve growled. "I told him you'd let Buck Ramsey have the run of the place around here. I complained to Sheriff Troy Hunt about it, too. About all either one of 'em gave me was sympathy. You let a murderer off scot-free by your cowardice, Sheriff Miller. Now he's prowling all over this neck of the woods. No tellin' who he'll kill next, or what sort of trouble he'll stir up." At that, Cleve opened the front of his coat to show

Gabe the gun he carried. "If Ramsey shows up around my place, I swear I'm gonna kill him. I told the judge what I'd do if Ramsey showed his face. Somebody has to act to protect the law-abiding citizens in this town. You've made it mighty damn plain you don't aim to protect us."

The rancher's threat pushed Gabe farther than he'd wanted to go. "What is it you're really afraid of, Mr. Wade? Is it Buck Ramsey? Or are you afraid of what he might find out?"

Cleve's eyelids tightened to mere slits. "Just what the hell do you mean by that, boy?" he demanded. He urged his horse closer to Gabe, his eyes alight with hatred, until their knees were almost touching.

Gabe met the big man's cold stare, although inside his heart was beating rapidly and his stomach knotted. "Only that you seem mighty concerned over Ramsey's whereabouts, when there isn't a scrap of proof that he killed anyone in Coryell County. Harvey Barnes told me just this morning that he remembered how you took quite a fancy to Anna Ramsey, back when she first came to town. I figure you're worried that Buck will find out how you used to pay social calls on his ma back then. He may want to ask you some questions about it."

Cleve's face turned crimson. He jutted his

jaw and leaned out of the saddle to be closer to Gabe. "I'm warnin' you, boy!" he snarled, gripping his reins angrily. "You're stickin' your nose where it don't belong. What happened between me an' the woman is none of your affair. You're walkin' out on some thin ice, thinkin' that tin badge gives you the right to poke into my personal business. If you've got good sense, you'll stay clear of me, or goddamn your miserable hide, I'll make you regret it!"

Responding to a rake of the rancher's spurs, the chestnut colt lunged off into a gallop.

CHAPTER 19

Martha was waiting supper for him, though it was well after dark when he arrived home. He'd done the chores by lantern light, chilled to the bone by long hours in the saddle and the search for the wagon. When he came to the house, Martha met him at the back door with a cup of coffee. For several minutes, the best he could manage was a word or two, standing close to the stove in his stocking feet, shivering like a newborn calf.

She prepared a bowl of stew for him and called him to the table. He left the warmth of the stove reluctantly to sit across from her.

"Your lips are blue," she said, smiling at him. "When you're able to talk, tell me what kept you. I know it must have been important, to keep you out in this horrible weather."

"I think I found Anna Ramsey's wagon," he began, spooning wonderfully warm stew into his mouth. He chewed thoughtfully a moment. "It's at the north end of the Wade ranch, what's left of it. Somebody burned it, trying to fix things so no one would ever find a trace."

Martha frowned. "How do you know it was Miz Ramsey's wagon?"

"Truth is, I don't for sure," he admitted. "But it's real strange that anybody would burn a wagon way out there, hidden in a brush pile right close to the falls. Peggy Sue told me about it. I rode out there to question Cleve about a few things. I talked to Harvey this morning. He told me how Cleve rode over to see Anna a bunch of times. Cleve wasn't at the ranch today. He'd ridden over to Gatesville to complain to Judge Green about how I'd let Buck Ramsey clear out of town without arresting him for Clarence's murder."

Martha's brow knitted. "Cleve Wade's a powerful man in this county. I hope he doesn't cause you to lose the sheriff's job."

He wagged his head. "I already talked to the judge about what's going on over here. Judge Green don't have all that high an opinion of Cleve, so don't worry."

"But I do worry, Gabe," she whispered, reaching across the table to touch his hand. "I'm worried about Buck Ramsey, about what might happen . . ."

"Ramsey doesn't worry me right now," he said. "If he wanted to kill me, he's already had plenty of chances. He wants to find out what happened to his brother and his ma, more than anything else. If he ever finds out who's responsible, that's when the trouble is gonna start. He suspects Cleve was behind it, and it's starting to look more and more like he's right. I found out something else, talking to Peggy Sue. There's a bunch of women's clothing up in their attic — she found them last spring. She thinks the dresses belonged to her ma, only what if they really were Anna Ramsey's? Only thing is, I don't know where to begin, trying to prove it."

"Did she say whether the clothes are still there?" Martha asked, unable to hide the growing excitement in her voice.

"No, I didn't ask. Peggy Sue got real unfriendly when I asked questions about finding that burned wagon. All the way home I've been thinking that maybe there's something up in that attic that would prove Anna was there at the ranch."

Martha had come to the edge of her chair. "How could you ever get up there to take a look without being seen? If Cleve's really guilty, he'd never allow you in the attic." She folded her arms across her chest, looking doubtful now. "Maybe the dresses do belong to Peggy Sue's mother. Maybe you're only jumping to conclusions."

"I know," he said quietly, stirring the con-

208

tents of his bowl absently. "But what if there's something up in the attic with Anna Ramsey's name on it, something no one could dispute? The only way I'll know for sure if Cleve is hiding evidence of his guilt up there is to figure a way to look for myself."

"It's far too dangerous," Martha warned, leaning forward again. "If he is guilty of anything . . ." She left the consequences unsaid, biting her lip briefly. "Do you really believe Cleve could have killed her? Or her son? Why would he do a thing like that? Harvey told you Cleve showed an interest in Anna. Why would he take her life if he had feelings for her?"

His supper forgotten, Gabe stared at the wall behind his wife, remembering his talk with Harvey. "Something Harvey said keeps coming back to me. He said he talked to Johnny one time about Cleve's visits to their cabin. Harvey remembers how the boy said his mother asked Cleve not to come around, only he did anyway. That doesn't make it sound like feelings went both ways between them."

"That still doesn't explain why he'd kill Johnny," Martha argued, "or why he would take Anna out to his ranch afterward, along with all her clothes. He'd have to be crazy to think he could keep her a prisoner out there, without anybody finding out. Peggy Sue would have known right away."

"She was off to a boarding school in Fort Worth. Cleve didn't bring Peggy Sue back until almost a year later. That's what she told me this morning."

"That's right!" Martha cried, almost shouting. "I remember."

Gabe toyed with his spoon, his appetite gone. "So it's quite possible Cleve could have forced Anna out to the ranch. Maybe something went wrong and he killed Johnny, then he had no choice but to . . . silence her, too."

"Or maybe," Martha said, "she grieved herself to death. If she got to where she wouldn't eat, I suppose she could have just wasted away."

He nodded thoughtfully, agreeing with the possibility. "It could have happened that way, I reckon. But if it did, it proves that Cleveland Wade is completely crazy. Only a crazy man would try to hold a woman prisoner like that."

"Love can make people crazy," Martha said softly. "I remember when poor old Windy Brown shot himself, right after his wife died. He was too grief stricken to live the rest of his life without her, folks said. Some called him crazy for doing a thing like that, but there were some who said they understood. Love can make people do crazy things."

"I've never done anything crazy on account

of being in love with you," he said, half joking, watching her expression.

"You most certainly have," she replied, pretending to pout. "Remember that time you swam all the way across the river to pick those blackberries for me? You kept bobbing up to the surface, sputtering like a fireplace bellows. I didn't know until two weeks later, when I told your ma about it, that you didn't know how to swim. You couldn't swim a lick, she said. Then she said it would have served you right if you'd drowned, pulling a crazy stunt like that."

"That was different," he protested unhappily, looking askance to hide his embarrassment. "Besides, the river wasn't all that deep in the first place. I can swim a little. I knew all along I could make it."

She giggled and caught his hand near the butter bowl, squeezing it gently. "You did it because you loved me — that's all I was saying. Some people do crazy things when they're in love."

Gabe frowned. "According to what Harvey remembered about what Johnny said, Anna didn't love Cleve at all. Sounds like she rejected his attentions."

Martha turned to look at the front door when she heard the dog growl on the porch. "What's making Red growl like that?" she wondered.

"I already fed him his supper . . ."

The dog's growl became a bark. The sound brought Gabe quickly to his feet, thinking that a fox might have come near the henhouse on a cold night, finding nothing else to eat. "I'll see what's got him worried," he said, clumping over to the wall where a shotgun hung on wooden pegs. "Probably just a fox after the chickens."

He was taking down the gun, listening to the big hound's bark become a savage snarl, when suddenly the front door burst open. Wheeling around, trying to bring the twelve-gauge to bear on the opening as quickly as he could, he heard Martha gasp as a shadowy figure entered the room, holding a pistol.

"Hold still," a harsh voice commanded, as the gun swung in Gabe's direction.

Gabe knew the voice before he could make out the identity of the intruder in the poor light from the lantern atop the table. He lowered the barrels of the shotgun to the floor and said, "It's all right, Martha. This is Buck Ramsey. I don't figure he aims to hurt us."

Ramsey nodded to Gabe, glancing briefly across the room at Martha. His pale eyes returned to Gabe's face. Little spits of snow swirled past him, driven through the open doorway by the wind, settling to the floor. "Step outside," he said above the dog's incessant barking. "Time you an' me had another talk."

Gabe shouted, "Be quiet, Red!" then he motioned Ramsey in. "Close the door. It's warmer here. My wife will give you some coffee."

Again, Ramsey looked at the woman while lowering the pistol to his side. "This oughta be private," he said coldly. "I want some straight answers about what you found out today."

"Martha knows everything," Gabe replied to Ramsey's objections, moving to close the door behind the gunman. "Sit down at the table. It'll take some time to tell you all of it. How did you know I'd done some looking around this afternoon?"

Ramsey merely grunted at first, keeping an eye on Gabe as the door was being shut. "I know," he said finally, sweeping his coat back to holster his gun when Gabe returned the twelve-gauge to its pegs.

As soon as Gabe looked at Martha, he saw the fear on her face. "It's okay," he said gently, coming over to her. "Pour Mr. Ramsey some coffee."

Tears welled in Martha's eyes. "Oh, Gabe," she whispered, clutching his shirtsleeve, her hands trembling. "Please ask him to leave."

The sound of Ramsey's spurs on the floor

warned that he approached the table. "Don't worry," Gabe told her quietly. "Pour the coffee and go to the bedroom. I promise everything will be all right."

She did as he asked, looking over her shoulder now and then as she poured Ramsey a cup of coffee, fear still written plainly across her face. She put the cup down on the table, then hurried into the bedroom. Once, before Gabe invited Ramsey to take a chair, he thought he heard the soft sounds of his wife crying.

"I went out to the Wade ranch today," Gabe began, pulling back his own chair.

"I followed you," the gunman told him, waiting for Gabe to sit, speaking without a trace of emotion. "I saw the wagon wheel down by the river. Couldn't figure what the hell you were doin', walkin' back and forth down there. I figure that was my ma's wagon. It was set afire so nobody would ever find it. Shows I was right all along. Wade killed my little brother. I figure he done the same to my ma."

"I can't prove it yet," Gabe protested, watching the gunman settle slowly into his seat. There was a catlike grace about Ramsey; he hardly ever wasted a movement. "I found out something else . . . a couple of things, really. Harvey Barnes told me that Cleve

214

might have tried to court your ma after a fashion, right after you left for the war. He also remembered that your brother didn't like it much."

"Figures," Ramsey growled, narrowing his eyes as he stared across the table.

"One more thing," Gabe went on. "Cleve's daughter told me about some dresses she found up in the attic of their house. Since her ma died giving birth to her, she thought it was unusual that Cleve kept her mother's dresses for so long. Downright unusual."

Very slowly, Ramsey's ice-blue eyes took on a strange, fiery glow. "You don't think they're her ma's dresses, do you?"

CHAPTER 20

The wagon bumped heavily over rocks hidden beneath the layer of snow, rattling, jostling them both on the spring-loaded seat. Wisps of frosty air curled from the mule's muzzle as it pulled the creaking wagon toward town. Martha sat beside him, dressed in her best dress, a bright-green woolen she decorated for Christmas with little bows fashioned from red ribbon. She held a cake pan on her lap, wrapped in a linen napkin covering frosted sugar cookies. Sometime during the night the snowfall had ended, leaving the Leon River valley with a crisp, cold morning without wind for the special Christmas services at the Eagle Springs Baptist Church. Gabe wore his only broadcloth suit, a threadbare black coat and trousers worn thin at the knees. He'd applied bootblack to his beat-up laced shoes, forgetting to wash his hands afterward, so that he'd gotten some of the black on his red bowtie. His starched white shirt collar cut into the flesh of his neck, though he suffered in silence.

The Christmas services were a special event. He could endure the choking collar for a few hours. For a time, he listened to the creak and groan of wagon axles. The grease in the greasepot had been too stiff in the cold to apply to the wheel hubs before they left. He glanced over at Martha, marveling at how pretty she looked, how her golden hair caught the morning sunlight.

"He is the most frightening man I've ever seen," Martha said, staring at the road ahead, remembering last night's uninvited visitor. "When he looked at me, it gave me shivers. He doesn't care about anyone, Gabe. He doesn't have any feelings. He reminds me of a wild animal . . . a wolf."

Gabe suppressed a chuckle, knowing how serious she was about disliking Ramsey. "Maybe it's because he lost his family. A thing like that could make a man turn hard on the surface."

Martha shook her head, like she knew there was more. "Alice said he killed a lot of people and robbed folks who were Union sympathizers. Back then, everybody talked about how he'd become an outlaw. If you ask me, he's capable of anything."

Gabe thought about it. "There was a war going on. Maybe he only did what the army wanted him to do. My pa said it was a terrible time. He hardly ever talked about it when he got back, but I heard him tell Uncle Jacob that Yankees weren't any different from the rest of us, and how he sure hated to shoot any of them just because they wore a blue uniform. Pa didn't know I was listening. He up'n cried, telling Uncle Jacob about it that time. I never saw him cry before."

"Buck Ramsey is different," Martha insisted. "He's got the coldest heart of any man I ever saw." She turned to Gabe, then grabbed his arm. Her eyes were moist when she spoke. "I'll say a prayer this morning that you don't ever have to have any dealings with him from here on. I got the shakes last night, just knowing he was there inside our house."

"You worry too much," he told her, flipping the reins over the mule's rump to hurry it along.

"I worry about you," she whispered, gripping his arm more tightly.

He waved her concerns away. "I can take care of myself," he said as the wagon rolled over the top of the ridge above Eagle Springs, where they could see columns of smoke rise from the chimneys across town. To take her mind off the meeting with Ramsey, he said, "Look yonder. Isn't it pretty, the way things are all covered with snow?" He turned to her, steadying himself on the swaying wagon seat, bending down to kiss her lightly on the mouth: "Merry Christmas," he whispered, grinning. "You look as pretty as a speckled pup in that green dress. If I wasn't already hitched, I'd ask you to marry me."

The noisy wagon started down the slope. East of the creek, they could see wagons and carriages, saddled horses and mules, gathered on the snowy church grounds. For the moment, Gabe forgot about everything else. The Christmas celebration would help take his mind off darker matters.

"All the womenfolk will be dressed fit to kill this morning," Martha promised, clutching the tin of cookies when the wagon jolted over a bump, her eyes glued to the assembling crowd milling back and forth near the front of the church. "There's sure to be plenty of gossip to go around, too."

"Alice will see to that," he offered glumly, guiding the mule around a snowdrift at the bottom of the grade. He glanced over at his wife. "Sure wish I could have bought you a new ready-made dress for Christmas. Maybe next year. I've got the feeling cotton is gonna sell high next fall."

She touched his sleeve gently and smiled. "I don't care about new dresses," she said. "Honest I don't."

He swung the wagon into the churchyard,

aiming for a vacant spot beside the Huffmans' wagon where he could tie the mule to an oak limb. Just as the wagon rattled to a halt, he heard Martha say, "That's strange, that Miz Culpepper wouldn't wave at me just now. She looked the other direction . . ."

"Maybe she didn't see you," he said, jumping down to help Martha from the seat. "I'll see to the mule, then I'll catch up to you."

Martha straightened the front of her dress, wiping away wrinkles. Balancing the tin of cookies, she started off through the snow as Gabe was giving the mule an ear of corn before tying it to the tree.

When the rope was secured he headed for the church, arriving at the same time Carl Jones and his wife reached the gathering.

"Mornin', Carl. Mornin', Miz Jones," he said, tipping his hat politely. "Merry Christmas to you."

Carl merely nodded, taking his wife's arm to usher her in another direction, causing Gabe to pause, puzzling over Carl's reaction. Unable to guess why Carl would ignore his greeting, he turned to a crowd of townspeople assembled near the church steps. At the center of the group, he saw Bonnie Cummings with her children gathered around her, suddenly remembering that he'd forgotten about the burial service for Clarence yesterday afternoon. He'd been so determined to find the remains of the wagon that the funeral completely slipped his mind.

"I'd better apologize," he said under his breath, heading over to speak to the Cummings family. A tall, gangly boy he didn't recognize stood beside Bonnie and he guessed it was Bobby, returned from Waco upon hearing of his father's death. Gabe had prepared a letter to the Thompson Gin, addressed to Bobby Cummings, although the stage hadn't come through town to pick it up yet.

He edged through the crowd, pausing long enough to tip his hat to Caleb and Vera Sikes, a farmer and his wife with whom he was barely acquainted. Caleb mumbled something and turned his back to Gabe, as though distracted. Gabe shook his head, wondering if it could be his imagination that folks were ignoring him. He walked up to Bonnie Cummings and pulled off his hat.

"Sorry I didn't make it back to town for the services, Miz Cummings," he said. "All this snow slowed me down. It was official business that kept me. Sorry I wasn't there."

Bonnie's eyes were brimming with tears. She nodded once and then put her arm around the boy standing beside her. "Bobby didn't get here till last night on account of the storm," she whimpered, on the brink of crying.

Gabe extended his hand to Bobby. "Sorry about what happened," he said, thinking how much the boy looked like Clarence.

Bobby took the handshake with little enthusiasm. "Ma tells me you still ain't arrested the feller who shot my pa," he said, making no effort to hide his anger.

"Nobody can say for sure who did it," Gabe explained. "There wasn't any witnesses."

A hush had fallen over the group around the Cummings family. Everyone listened to the exchange between Gabe and Bobby.

"That ain't what I was told, Sheriff," the boy replied. "Will Jameson saw Buck Ramsey ridin' hell-for-leather away from our place that mornin'. I say that's proof enough that Ramsey done it, only it don't appear it's enough to satisfy you."

Someone pushed through the assembled bystanders, taking Gabe's attention from the boy momentarily before he could reply. Cleveland Wade, dressed in a tailored brown riding suit and stovepipe boots, walked directly in front of Gabe and halted abruptly, a look of scorn on his face. Then he turned to the crowd around them and spoke in a crisp, angry voice.

"This sheriff you folks elected has allowed a murderer to run loose in our midst! He hasn't got the backbone to arrest the man who gunned down Clarence Cummings. Clarence

222

was murdered in cold blood, and this boy won't lift a finger to put the killer in jail. I hope you all remember that, come election time!"

A murmur spread through the bystanders. Cleve glared at the faces around him, then he aimed a withering stare down at Gabe.

"So, what do you have to say for yourself, Sheriff?" he demanded. "Tell these good taxpayers why you haven't arrested Buck Ramsey."

Silence followed Cleve's angry outburst. Gabe swallowed, trying to calm a tremor in his hands. "Because there's no proof that Ramsey did it," Gabe replied. "I already told you that. When I can prove who committed the murder, I'll make an arrest. That's how the law works, Mr. Wade. You can't charge a man with a crime without any proof."

The big rancher's expression was clearly one of disdain. "Then maybe you can explain why you're looking for your proof out at my ranch, Sheriff Miller. My daughter tells me you were out there yesterday, asking questions about me. I take that as a personal insult! Everyone in this end of Coryell County knows me as an honest citizen, a taxpayer." He pointed to Bonnie Cummings. "I called this woman's husband my friend. He was a good neighbor. It's no secret that I made Clarence a loan the

223

day before he was murdered, so he could pay his back taxes. And now you have the gall to accuse me publicly of killing a neighbor, and a friend."

Gabe hooked his thumbs in the waistband of his trousers to keep his hands from shaking. He looked Cleve in the eye. "I haven't accused you of anything, Mr. Wade. I was only trying to find out what happened to Anna Ramsey ten years ago, and who might have killed her son. That's the reason Buck is here. He's after revenge, and I'm trying to get to the bottom of things so the law can handle it proper."

Cleve leaned closer to Gabe's face, his lips drawn back in a snarl. "Then you're accusing me of those crimes too," he said. "I won't stand for it! I'm warning you, boy — don't ever show your face on my property again. You're nothing but a young fool with a badge pinned to your chest. I hope the decent citizens of this town realize the mistake they made, electing you sheriff."

Whispered voices sounded all around Gabe, though he couldn't quite hear what was being said. He was set to argue the point further with Cleve, when Reverend Sims hurried into the circle of bystanders with a worried look on his face.

"Now, now, gentlemen," the preacher said softly, looking from one man to the other. "It's

224

a special Sunday today, the Sunday before Christmas. Let's not spoil our joyous celebration with disagreement. Please come inside so the services may begin. My wife is ready at the pump organ. We should all share the true spirit of the season today. Come to worship and forget your differences in the name of the Lord."

Cleve's expression softened when Peggy Sue came to his side. She took his arm. "Let's go inside," she whispered without giving Gabe so much as a sideways glance.

Cleve allowed himself to be led away to the church steps. The others followed without a word, leaving Gabe standing alone where the confrontation had occurred. He took a deep breath, sure that his face was red, then heard someone sobbing softly behind him.

When he turned around, he saw Martha with her hands pressed to her face. The tin of sugar cookies had fallen near her feet, spilling frosted cookies over the snow. He rushed over to her and put his arms around her, feeling her shoulders shaking in his embrace. "There now," he said softly. "No reason to cry. Folks are upset because of what happened to Clarence. Cleve is only trying to make things worse."

She looked up at him, with tears streaming down her face. "No one will even talk to me," she cried, as though begging for understanding. "Alice would hardly say more than hello. She acted like I wasn't there. What's wrong, Gabe? Why is everyone treating us like this?"

He held her close, thinking of an answer. Inside the church, the old pump organ wheezed into a hymn. Soon, voices joined the music, while Gabe and Martha stood alone in the snowy churchyard. "I can't really explain it," he began, talking quietly near her ear. "I reckon folks are scared. Some of 'em are scared of Buck Ramsey and what they think he might do to innocent people if someone happened to get in his way. Others are afraid of Cleve Wade and the influence his money buys him. Cleve likes to bully folks in order to get what he wants." Here, Gabe paused to take a breath, looking up at the morning sky. "And I think Cleve's scared too, scared that I'll discover something that'll expose him for who he really is — a murderer, a man who thought he'd gotten away with killing three times."

A moment later Martha stopped sobbing. She sniffled, then looked up at him with teary, red-rimmed eyes. "What if you're wrong, Gabriel?" she whispered.

He didn't have an answer for her. He could only shrug and try to comfort her. "Let's go inside," he told her gently. "We can sit in

226

the back pew, where hardly anybody will notice. It's Christmastime, and I won't let anybody spoil our Christmas for us." He smiled, and bent down to kiss her cheek. "Besides, you're the prettiest girl in the whole county and I won't miss the chance to show you off in front of everybody. Take hold of my arm, Martha Elizabeth. We're gonna walk inside that church with our heads held proud."

He let go of her and knelt down to pick up the fallen cookies, dusting them off one at a time to rid them of snow. When he came to the last one, he grinned and stuck the whole thing in his mouth in one big bite, stretching his cheeks as he stood up beside her.

The sight of his swollen face made her laugh a little. She dried her eyes with the back of her hand and took his arm to walk beside him to the church steps. Inside, a chorus of voices accompanied the organ in a rendition of "Silent Night." Before Gabe opened the door, Martha started to sing.

CHAPTER 21

Gabe was dozing. Now and then he'd catch himself and straighten his spine against the back of the hard wooden pew, forcing his eyes open a few moments longer while Reverend Sims droned on about the birth of the baby Jesus. The back of the church was pleasantly warm, so close to the big iron stove in a rear corner. It was a struggle to stay awake, until he heard the sound of a running horse outside.

The pounding hoofbeats stopped near the church steps, then heavy boots raced to the doors. A door swung open, interrupting the preaching. Will Jameson stood in the doorway, seeking someone in the congregation.

"Sheriff!" Will blurted out, sounding out of breath when he found Gabe at the back of the room. "Come quick, an' bring a gun! Buck Ramsey just broke into Cleve Wade's house — kicked the door in. I saw the whole thing from the bunkhouse. I saddled a horse an' came to town quick as I could."

Gabe bolted to his feet, wide awake now.

He spoke to Martha quickly before starting toward the door. "I'll have to unharness the mule — the wagon's too slow. Wait here for me. I'll be back as soon as I can."

She made a grab for his arm, though he left much too quickly. "Please be careful, Gabe!" she cried as he hurried out of the church.

Running through the snow, he stumbled once and almost fell flat before regaining his balance. When he reached the mule and began removing the harness, he heard running feet coming toward him. Expecting Martha, he was surprised to see Peggy Sue racing over to him, her face flush from the run through powdery drifts.

"Take my horse, Gabriel!" she shouted, pointing to the big sorrel stallion she'd been riding the day before. "It'll take that mule all day to get out there. Pa and Will said they're coming right behind you. Pa's mad as all get-out. Please don't let that outlaw shoot my pa!"

Gabe glanced across the grounds to the sorrel stud. "It'll be faster," he agreed. "I've got to stop by the office to pick up my gun. Try to keep your pa here, Peggy Sue. He's no match for Ramsey with a six-gun, and with a temper like your pa's, there's sure to be big trouble."

The girl nodded as tears began to fill her

eyes. "Why would Buck Ramsey break into our house like that?" she asked, her voice breaking a little.

"I think I know why," he told her quietly, starting for the horse. "Those dresses you told me about up in the attic — I think Ramsey believes they belonged to his mother . . ."

Suddenly, Peggy Sue's eyes rounded with surprise. "You told him!" she cried, aiming an accusing finger at Gabe. "You told him about that old trunk I found!"

There wasn't time to explain it properly, why he'd mentioned the clothing to Ramsey. "I'll tell you why when I get back," he said over his shoulder. "Just keep your pa here as long as you can."

Untying the stud, he climbed aboard, finding the girl's stirrups much too short. He heeled the horse to a lope down Main Street, knowing that the only way to stop Ramsey from taking anything from the Wade ranch would require a gun. Ramsey had gone too far this time, breaking into the house while the Wades were at church. He'd taken the law into his own hands, and it was the sheriff's responsibility to stop him — if Gabe could accomplish it without losing his own life in the process.

He reined the stud to a bounding halt in front of the office and jumped down to unlock the door. Inside, he took the gun and holster from his desk drawer and ran back out to the horse. Looping the gun belt around the saddlehorn, he mounted and urged the sorrel to a run toward the outskirts of town, feeling the rush of cold air against his cheeks when the horse gathered speed. With his heart pounding, dreading the moment when he confronted Ramsey, he gave the stallion its head and settled against the cantle for a long ride, a ride that could be his last if he let Ramsey have the advantage. Once, at the top of a ridge above Eagle Springs, he glanced over his shoulder, hoping that Peggy Sue could somehow manage to keep Cleve at the church long enough for him to get to the ranch first. For now, no one followed him, lessening the chances that Gabe might be caught in a deadly crossfire.

His hands and face felt frozen by the time he galloped the winded horse up the lane toward the house. He took some comfort in the discovery that Ramsey's roan horse was nowhere in sight. The ride out to the ranch had taken long enough that Ramsey had had time to find what he was looking for, if Gabe could count on a piece of luck. Along the way, Gabe had cursed himself silently for telling a dangerous man like Ramsey about Peggy Sue's discovery until he had proof that the dresses belonged to Anna. Now it appeared that Gabe's wagging tongue and nothing more than a wild guess were about to set off an explosion that would shatter the quiet of a peaceful Sunday morning in the Leon River valley. Cleve Wade would be furious, demanding Ramsey's arrest for the break-in. Gabe would be caught in a crossfire between them, or forced to take on Ramsey in an attempt to arrest him.

He pulled the stud to a halt in front of the house and leapt from the saddle. Running up the porch steps, he checked his back-trail and found it clear. The front door stood ajar. Clutching his pistol, Gabe entered the house, glancing up at the ceiling, toward the attic. If Ramsey was still inside, he would be up there. Moving softly on his toes, Gabe started for a stairway at the end of a shadowy hallway, listening to the beating of his heart.

He took the steps two at a time, his thumb resting on the hammer of the .44, eyes glued to the top of the stairwell and the second floor. His breathing grew short, labored, a mixture of exertion and fear by the time he reached the landing. Despite the chill in the house, beads of sweat formed on his face and his hand grew clammy around the walnut pistol grips. The sounds of his shoes on the stairs echoed like thunder in the silence, until he reached the top of the stairway, where he hesitated, listening for the slightest noise.

The hallway at the top of the steps was dark, painted with deep shadows where a man could be hidden, waiting for him. Gabe wondered where the entrance to the attic was, knowing the risks of plodding around the second story across wood floors, making noises that would alert Ramsey to his presence. Tightening his grip on the gun, he moved forward again on the balls of his feet, pausing now and then to watch and listen.

Slowly, moving from dark room to dark room where thick curtains held out the sun's light, he inspected three empty bedrooms briefly, until he came to a fourth room with a sewing table and a lone straight-backed chair. A musty smell greeted his nostrils as he crept inside, leveling the pistol in front of him. A shaft of sunlight from an opening in the heavy drapes revealed a ladder in a back corner, leading to an opening in the ceiling. The hole in the roof was dark. "He probably isn't up there now," he whispered. "There's no light."

He moved softly to the ladder and stuck the pistol in his waistband, then began a slow ascent. The rungs creaked under his weight, until his head rose above the attic floor. The attic space was as black as pitch. Climbing carefully, he continued up the ladder, pausing again when he could stand on the attic floor.

For a few moments he waited for his eyes to adjust to the absence of light. He saw the dim outline of a small table close by, and when he moved over to it, his fingers touched a candle, seated in a small metal holder. He smelled burnt wax. The candle had been extinguished not long ago. And beside it, he found a box of sulfur matches. He understood that striking a match would make him an easy target for Ramsey, if the gunman waited for him in the darkness. Yet some inner sense told Gabe that he was alone, so he took out a match and struck it on the tabletop.

Shadows danced across the attic space in the flicker of fire from the match. He lit the candle and let out a sigh when more light revealed that no one else was there. Now he examined his surroundings closely. At once his gaze fell on a battered wooden trunk, halfway across the floor, its top hanging open. Discarded clothing lay all around the trunk, as though someone had removed things hurriedly. Picking up the candle, Gabe started over to the trunk.

When he held the light close to the trunk, he noticed its rusted hasp and hinges. But then his eye was drawn to the bottom of it, where the golden glow of the candle revealed a bundle of yellowed envelopes, tucked between a pair of badly worn high-button women's shoes. He bent down to retrieve the letters. Frowning in the bad light, he read the name scrawled across the front of the first envelope.

"Mrs. Anna Marie Ramsey," he whispered breathlessly, *"in care of Huffman's General Store, Eagle Springs, Texas."* For one brief moment, it seemed his heartbeat stopped altogether. "She was here," he added almost soundlessly. "This was her trunk." He noted the sender's name at the top of the envelope: *From Captain Buckingham Ramsey, Hood's Fifth Texas Cavalry, CSA.* Gabe took a deep breath.

It seemed that a thousand tangled thoughts entered his brain at once. The letter was proof that Anna Ramsey had come to the Wade ranch, most likely on the night her son was killed, against her will. Gabe could only guess what happened to her after that, but it was almost certain that she died here, perhaps even by the hand of Cleveland Wade. With Peggy Sue off at boarding school, no one else would have known he had an unwilling guest in the house, if he kept Anna locked in a room, out of sight. Cleve had covered his tracks very well that night. The trunk was the only telltale clue he'd left behind to point to his guilt.

The flame flickered, revealing something

else at the bottom of the trunk, something made of metal. Gabe stuck the bundle of letters in his coat pocket and bent down to see what had caught his attention.

He picked up a faded tintype in a dusty bronze frame, the likeness of a woman, smiling back at him. A mane of flowing dark hair touched the woman's waist. She wore a lacy white wedding dress with a buttoned collar reaching her chin. Her skin was like smooth cream, flawless, covering high cheekbones. She was easily one of the most beautiful women Gabe had ever seen, with striking good looks of a kind that drew your attention and held it. He found it easy to understand how a man could fall in love with this woman. Then he looked closely at her eyes, finding them the same pale color as those of her son. She was so pretty, he thought, staring at the picture. But a man would have to be plumb crazy to think he could keep her a prisoner out here, like he owned her.

He tucked the tintype into an inside pocket of his coat, then loosened his bowtie. Time I took this over to Judge Green, he thought, snuffing out the candle. This will be enough to issue an arrest warrant for Cleveland Wade. There's still a heck of a lot more to be proved. Maybe Miz Hawkins will talk, when she knows Cleve can't hurt her from a jail cell.

He returned the candle to the table and started back down the ladder, wondering where Ramsey might be now. Ramsey knew what the trunk contained, and if Gabe was any great shakes as a guesser, Ramsey would be headed for a showdown with the man who was responsible for the death of his family.

Hurrying down the stairs, Gabe wondered if he stood any chance of stopping the killing. Ramsey wasn't the type to listen to much argument. But if Gabe could convince him that Cleve Wade's murder trial would serve the cause of justice, perhaps even a hardened killer like Buck Ramsey would be satisfied to see Cleve go to a hangman's gallows to pay for his crimes.

Out on the front porch, Gabe's eyes hurt when sunlight almost blinded him, reflected off the snow. Only after he'd mounted the sorrel stud was he able to see the ruts back to Eagle Springs clearly. The road was empty. Peggy Sue had apparently been able to keep her father and Will Jameson from following Gabe out to the ranch. Now, if he could only get back to town in time, there was a chance he could talk Ramsey out of killing Cleve. Everything depended on the speed and endurance of the horse between his knees.

He reined the stud around and drummed his heels into its sides, bending into the rush of cold air when the sorrel lunged to a run. The tall stallion's head bobbed up and down with the power of its gallop as it carried Gabe off the hilltop, toward town.

CHAPTER 22

The stud galloped tirelessly along the wagon ruts. Gabe tried to read the snow for recent tracks leading back to town, but the task proved to be impossible. Some of the hoofprints had been left behind by Will Jameson's horse. Gabe halfway expected to run headlong into Cleve and Will somewhere on the road, although for now he rode alone through empty, tree-studded hills, listening to the drumming of the horse's hooves.

He felt sorry for Peggy Sue, whose comment about the dresses had provided the missing pieces to the puzzle, exposing her father's guilt. A casual remark she made about what she found up in the attic had provided the key to solving the ten-year-old mystery, but it would be a burdensome agony for a loving daughter, even though none of what happened was her fault.

The sorrel raced down an incline leading to the bottom of a ravine where a thick stand of live oaks grew close to the road. Gabe's

239

mind was on the envelopes and the tintype in his pocket, thus he paid little attention to the trees. Idly watching the road ahead, he was startled when a horse and rider lunged across his path. The first thing he noticed was that Cleveland Wade was aiming a pistol at him.

"Whoa, there!" Gabe cried, sawing back on the stud's reins in the same instant he saw Cleve. Gabe's horse came to a sliding stop, sending a shower of snowflakes from its hooves. "Why are you pointing that gun at me?" he asked, for the moment bewildered by the rancher's actions.

"Where the hell's Ramsey?" Cleve snapped, boring through Gabe with a look.

"He wasn't there when I got to the house. I'd guess he cleared out just before I arrived."

Cleve appeared to notice the bulge in Gabe's coat pocket just then, before his hard stare returned to Gabe's face. "Maybe I've got it figured otherwise," he said. "I figure you ran from him again like a yellow-livered coward, same as you did the first time."

Gabe stiffened in the saddle. "You're wrong," he replied evenly. "Ramsey was gone when I got there. The door was left open, and there was a ladder in the opening to the attic. He'd been inside, I reckon, but he's gone now."

At the mention of the attic, Cleve's eyes returned briefly to the bulge in Gabe's pocket. "What's that in your coat?" he demanded, raising the barrel of his gun slightly.

The question caught Gabe off guard, with his attention fixed on the pistol muzzle. Now his thoughts raced for an answer, one that might buy a little time. "Official county business," he said. "I'm taking some papers over to Judge Green."

"Like hell," Cleve declared, edging his horse closer to Gabe's, leveling the gun in his fist. "Not until you prove those papers don't belong to me. I knew all along I should have destroyed her things, but I couldn't. Hand 'em over!"

"I won't do it," Gabe insisted. "Now holster that gun, Mr. Wade. You're interfering with the lawful duty of a peace officer. These papers are headed over to the judge."

For a moment Cleve sat his horse in silence, still aiming the pistol at Gabe's belly. Then he snarled, "You're forcin' my hand, boy," and quickly swept the ravine with nervous glances in every direction before his thumb cocked the hammer of his gun. "Looks like we're all alone out here," he added, lowering his voice. "I told Will to stay with my daughter, so it's just you an' me, Sheriff Miller. I reckon those papers are mine, and I'm afraid

I can't let you keep them. You've been up in my attic, stickin' your nose where it don't belong. Everybody's gonna be real upset to hear that Buck Ramsey shot you. I'll tell 'em I found you out here, lyin' in the snow with a bullet in you. And then I'll get that murder warrant for Ramsey, like I wanted all along."

Suddenly, Gabe's heart was hammering. He harbored no doubt that Cleve meant every word of what he said. Without the letters in Gabe's pocket, nearly everyone in Coryell County would believe Cleve's version of the story, even if Ramsey lived long enough to say what he had found in the attic. By then Cleve would have destroyed all the evidence. Gabe summoned all his courage to frame his next question, realizing he couldn't possibly reach inside his coat for his own gun before Cleve pulled the trigger. "One more killing won't matter, will it?" he asked. "By my count, you've already killed three people."

Cleve blinked, then a sardonic grin widened his mouth. "Three? I didn't kill the woman," he said. "I loved her. Everything would have been fine if that boy hadn't got in the way. After I brought her here I treated her like a queen. But she kept pining for that boy. Wouldn't eat anything. Got down to skin an' bones. One morning, I found her dead in bed. I buried her behind the house. I would have done anything for her."

Hoping to buy more time, Gabe asked, "I still don't understand why you shot the kid."

Again, Cleve checked their surroundings, making sure they were alone. "I don't suppose it matters if I tell you. The boy, he tried to stop me from seein' Anna that night. Met me with a shotgun, comin' up from the creek. He said he'd shoot me if I didn't leave her alone. He cocked the damn gun an' aimed for my head. I shot him down in self-defense, but especially since there were no witnesses I knew everybody was gonna blame me for killin' a little boy. So I made Anna pack up some things and I took her out to the ranch. I kept tryin' to explain that I didn't have a choice when Johnny aimed for me. I loved that woman, only she wouldn't listen to me. And I damn sure couldn't let her leave, or I'd wind up in jail. That's the long and the short of it, Sheriff Miller. Too bad Buck Ramsey came back and stirred up everything."

Gabe hoped he could keep Cleve talking long enough for Ramsey to show up, looking for Cleve. "Why did you kill Clarence?" Gabe asked, figuring his best chance lay in somehow distracting Cleve long enough to get at the revolver hidden in his waistband.

"Clarence saw me drive Anna out to the ranch that night. I paid him to keep quiet about it. When Ramsey showed up asking questions, Clarence got scared. He was afraid Ramsey meant to kill him, so I couldn't trust him anymore. As it is, everyone in town believes Ramsey shot Clarence. Everyone except you, that is." Cleve's expression hardened. "You're wastin' my time with all these damn questions, boy."

It was then Gabe knew time had run out. Cleve's trigger finger tightened, and in the same instant, Gabe was clawing for the gun hidden inside his coat. He had his hand around the pistol grips, when an explosion rocked the silence. The bullet from Cleve's gun slammed into Gabe's ribs with the force of a mule's kick and he was torn from the saddle, falling backward over the stallion's rump. White-hot pain shot through his left side as he went tumbling into the snow, landing on his back with such suddenness that all the air was driven from his lungs. He couldn't breathe, and his ears were ringing from the gun blast. Dimly, he caught a glimpse of the sorrel as it bounded away from the noise, trailing its reins. Things had happened too quickly — there hadn't been time to think about what was taking place. Staring up at the sky, with pain knifing through him, Gabe wondered if he might be dying.

Someone bent over him. He saw Cleve's

face, and at the same moment, he felt something wet and warm flow down his ribs. In a dark corner of his brain he knew blood was draining from the bullet hole in his side and yet he was helpless to do anything about it, his arms and legs unable to move. Then a black fog swirled before his eyes, encircling him. He was losing consciousness rapidly. A groan whispered from his chest before his eyelids closed. It was as if a gentle wind lifted him off the ground, carrying him away.

The darkness grayed. He'd been vaguely aware of strange dreams. More than anything else, he tried to focus his thoughts on his beloved Martha, wondering if the dark void he found himself in was the pathway toward hell the Reverend Sims talked about, the first place sinners went after death occurs.

The fog around him brightened. He thought he heard a distant voice. "Who's there?" he asked. "Where am I?"

Gradually, a shape appeared in the mist. He saw a man's face, although at first, he did not recognize him. Then a voice spoke plainly. "You've lost a lot of blood."

He tried to clear his vision. The image before him grew sharper. A man with a handlebar mustache looked down at him, a man with strange pale eyes. "It hurts," he said, as a pain in his side became sharper, more distinct.

"I reckon it should," the man above him replied, frowning some. "It made one hell of a hole, but it passed through clean. You'll live, if I can stop the bleeding."

Very slowly at first, Gabe began to remember the face he saw before him now. "You're Buck Ramsey," he mumbled, having trouble forming words. He took a deep breath, wincing from the pain as he came full awake. "Cleve Wade shot me. He admitted killing your brother, and Clarence Cummings. He claims he didn't kill your ma — she died of grief. He said he loved her."

"I had most of it figured," Ramsey said, opening the buttons on Gabe's shirt. "Lie still. I'm gonna put a strip of cloth over the wound, then I'll get you over my saddle. You need a doctor."

"Where's Cleve?" he managed to ask, feeling faint again, though his mind was still clear.

Ramsey's face showed nothing when he said, "It don't matter now. I reckon I missed him somewhere on the trail. Wherever the bastard is, I'll find him. First thing is to get you where it's warm and stop this bleedin'."

Gabe remembered what he found inside the trunk. "There were some letters up in the attic, and a tintype of your ma. I was taking them over to Gatesville, to Judge Green."

Ramsey merely grunted at first, pulling Gabe's shirt away from his side. "You won't need that judge when I'm done with Wade," he said quietly. "An undertaker, maybe."

Gabe started to protest. "I've got enough to send Cleve to prison . . . most likely to a hangman's noose. Let the law handle it."

"I never take chances anymore, son," he said. "You took a chance with Wade, and this is what it got you. I'll have to hand you one thing, Gabriel Miller — you may be a little short on talent with a gun, but you're longer on nerve than I figured. I'll take care of Wade, and when I'm done with him, you can do whatever you want with the body. He'll pay for what he did to my brother and my ma."

Ramsey was gone before Gabe could argue it further, the gunman's heavy boots and spurs crunching through the snow. Moments later he returned with a strip of shirttail, then he knelt and tied it gently around Gabe's ribs.

"I'll hoist you up in front of me," he said when the bandage was tied in place. "It's gonna hurt some, but it's the only way to get you to town."

Gabe felt his wound gingerly, moving his fingertips along his ribs. "I can make it," he said. Then his hand touched the tintype in his coat pocket. "I found this likeness of your ma up there too," he added. "Cleve wanted the letters, but he must have missed the tintype. She was real pretty."

"I saw the tintype," Ramsey replied. "I left everything, so when the law searched Wade's house, they'd find evidence of his guilt, even though by then he'd be stone-cold dead."

Gabe attempted to sit up, but pain drove him back to the ground. "They'll only send you back to prison," he told Ramsey with his teeth clenched. "My way is better. They'll hang him for sure if he stands trial."

Ramsey lifted Gabe by the shoulders, holding him upright until his legs were steady. "You're wastin' your breath, son," he said in a soft voice. "Nothing you can say will stop me from killing him. I've had a long time to think about the consequences. I'll take my chances, bein' on the run. Now put your arm around my neck. It ain't far to my horse, a step or two."

Gabe was too weak to argue the point then. Unintentionally, he looked down and saw blood all over the snow where he'd been lying. Steadying himself against Ramsey, he started slowly toward the blue roan gelding, closing his eyes when weakness threatened to buckle his knees. Though his head reeled from pain and blood loss, he found himself thinking about the contradictions in Ramsey's charac-

248

ter. His record proved that he was a hardened killer, yet he showed real compassion toward Gabe.

With Ramsey's help, Gabe fitted an unsteady boot into a stirrup, then swung painfully over the saddle. Ramsey got up behind him, holding him atop the roan. The gelding was reined south, toward Eagle Springs, moving off at a walk. Gabe gritted his teeth, fighting to remain conscious, closing his mind to the pain.

CHAPTER 23

He kept slipping in and out of consciousness despite his best efforts to stay awake. It seemed like forever before the roan crested the hill above the Eagle Springs Baptist Church. Gabe saw their wagon in the churchyard. Half a dozen more were still parked below the trees. Little knots of people stood in the snow, talking, he supposed, lingering long after the service and Christmas party afterward. The gathering was an annual event, lasting into the middle of the afternoon. Then a sudden thought occurred to him that sent a wave of fear through his addled brain, bringing him fully conscious. What if Cleve Wade happened to be in the group down at the church now? The showdown between him and Ramsey could take place right here and now. Cleve had left Gabe for dead back there — the rancher was in for a pair of unwanted surprises if he was among the folks Gabe could see from the top of the hill.

"Cleve's liable to be there," Gabe groaned,

gripping the saddlehorn with all his strength to stay aboard the roan as it started down the gentle slope.

"Then I won't have to go looking for him," Ramsey said tonelessly.

"Don't do this, Ramsey. Let me handle it," Gabe went on, clamping his teeth together when the rocking motion of the horse's gait worsened the ache in his side, noticing from the corner of his eye that Ramsey suddenly swept the tail of his duster behind the butt of his holstered pistol.

"He'll die at the end of a rope if you'll listen to reason," Gabe protested, growing weaker.

"Save your breath, Sheriff," Ramsey whispered hoarsely. "I've had a little taste of how the law works. Stay out of it."

"You'll be making a mistake if you kill him," Gabe warned. "You'll be a wanted man the rest of your life, or you'll die in prison."

Gabe couldn't be sure, but it sounded like Ramsey chuckled.

"Seems like I've been a hunted man almost every day since I been grown," he said. "I reckon it's fair to say I'm accustomed to it. The law you represent can't touch me below the Mexican border."

The horse reached the bottom of the hill, forcing Gabe's attention to the people gathered near the church, seeking Cleve among them.

Sunlight reflecting off the snow played tricks with his eyes, until his gaze wandered to the church steps, where the Reverend Sims stood with Peggy Sue Wade, Harlan Huffman, and a towering figure in a brown riding suit and flat-brimmed hat.

"Yonder he is," Gabe said softly. "He'll know he's cornered. I sure wish you'd let me try to handle it my way . . ."

Ramsey reined the gelding to the edge of the open ground surrounding the church. He halted the horse abruptly beside a tree and swung down. "Stay here," he said, giving Gabe a sideways glance that conveyed strong meaning.

With his coattail tucked behind his gun, Ramsey started across the snow toward Cleve Wade. Every face near the church was watching him. People began to back away, some of the women hurrying to safety with the hems of their skirts lifted. A few of the men looked at each other before joining the women to take flight. Reverend Sims seemed undecided, then took Peggy Sue by the arm and pulled her toward the doors of the church.

Gabe saw Martha running in his direction and he desperately wanted her out of the way of flying bullets. As quickly as he could, he pulled his right leg over the gelding's rump and then stepped gingerly to the ground. For a fleeting second he held onto the saddlehorn, waiting for a wave of nausea and dizziness to pass. Then he pushed away from the roan and started toward his wife, shouting, "Please get out of the way!"

Martha rushed to his side, ignoring the warning. She had already seen the blood. "What happened, Gabe?" she whimpered, taking his arm as tears flooded down her cheeks.

"Cleve tried to kill me," he replied, staggering over to a nearby tree to support himself. "Now Ramsey's gonna have his revenge and I can't stop it. Get behind this tree. I've got to make one last try at talking Ramsey out of this."

"Please don't go," Martha cried, refusing to let go of his arm.

He pushed her hand away roughly and half stumbled away from the oak trunk, trying to keep his feet under him for the hundred-yard walk to the church steps where Cleve stood, watching Ramsey draw nearer. The front of Cleve's coat hung open, revealing the butt of his gun in the cross-pull holster buckled across his belly. When Cleve noticed Gabe, the color drained from his face. Then his eyes went back to Ramsey as he spread his feet slightly apart and went into a battle-ready crouch.

Before Gabe could take more than a dozen

steps away from the tree, Ramsey halted. A deadly silence gripped the onlookers hidden behind parked wagons and tree trunks. For a time, the only sound came from Gabe's boots as he plodded unsteadily through the snow to reach the two men. Then suddenly, Ramsey's harsh voice echoed like a peal of rolling thunder.

"Cleve Wade!" he shouted, aiming a steely look across the distance between him and his adversary. "You killed my family ten years ago! Today's the day you pay the price!"

Cleve's right hand was poised near the butt of his gun. He glared back at Ramsey. "You're crazy," he said, jutting his square jaw.

Gabe continued to stumble and stagger toward them, almost blinded by pain, clutching the wound in his side.

"I've seen the proof!" Ramsey growled. "I saw the letters up in the attic. You kept my ma a prisoner out there, you bastard, until she died of grief after you killed Johnny. Now it's your turn to know what dying is like. Go for your gun! I'll give you the first pull."

"It's a bluff!" Cleve snapped. "You won't gun me down in front of all these witnesses."

"You're dead wrong, Wade! Reach for that gun or I'll kill you where you stand! Either way, you're a dead man!"

Gabe had closed the distance to twenty

yards. He opened his mouth and yelled, "Stop!" then saw Cleve's hand flash toward the opening in his coat. "No!" he cried. His boot toe caught on something hidden in the snow and he started to fall forward, knowing he was just seconds too late. As Gabe fell, the scene unfolding before him took on a syruplike slowness, as though he saw it in a dream.

Ramsey's hand came up filled with iron. The roar of his gun seemed to shake the ground. A bright yellow muzzle flash spat forth from the barrel of his .44, accompanying the resounding clap of the shot. The explosion echoed back and forth from the surrounding forest as Gabe was landing face-first in the snow.

Looking up, he saw Cleve flinch and stagger backward, eyes wide with surprise and sudden pain. His gun dropped near his feet, then his powerful hands clawed his shirt front. A shower of crimson spray flew from the back of his coat, pattering down on the packed snow behind him. For a moment, his knees sagged, then he righted himself and looked down at his blood-soaked hands.

A curl of blue gunsmoke wafted away from the muzzle of Ramsey's gun. It lifted lazily in the still air, spreading, rising toward the sky. Ramsey stood rock-still, watching Cleve struggle to remain on his feet. Someone near one of the wagons gasped. A woman's voice exclaimed, "Dear God!"

"No!" Gabe cried again, softer this time, spitting out a mouthful of snow. His fall had taken his breath away and the sound he made was like the croak of a bullfrog. His eyes were locked on Cleve. Slowly, the rancher's knees gave way and he knelt on a patch of bloody snow, grimacing, both hands gripping the hole in his chest, trying to stem the flow.

Ramsey lowered his gun and started toward his dying victim, boots crunching softly, spurs muffled by snow. He stopped a few feet from Cleve and stared down at him. "We're even now, you son of a bitch," he snarled.

Peggy Sue screamed from the front of the church, trying to break away from the Reverend Sims's grip on her arm to rush to her father's side. The preacher held on and tried to comfort her.

"There's nothing you can do for him now," Sims said.

Cleve looked up from his wound. His mouth dropped open, then his lips moved soundlessly as bloody spittle poured out, dribbling down his chin, spilling down the front of his coat and shirt. He rocked on his knees, caught himself without ever taking his eyes from Ramsey, and fell forward, landing with a heavy thump, facedown, near Ramsey's feet.

Gabe witnessed the duel's final moments without moving, watching the grisly end while lying on his stomach. He heard footsteps running toward him and turned his head. Martha rushed to his side and knelt, sobbing softly. "I'm okay," he told her in a throaty whisper.

More footsteps approached. When Gabe looked up, he saw Ramsey standing over him.

"Get this man to a doctor," Ramsey said to Martha. "He's lost a lot of blood."

It was the gentlest voice Gabe had ever heard Ramsey use. One word lingered in Gabe's thoughts. "At least you didn't call me a boy this time," he muttered, trying for a grin despite the throbbing in his ribs.

The gunman nodded once. "You proved to me and everybody else in this one-horse town that you're no boy. Fact is, you've got more guts than most men I've known. You're a hell of a good sheriff, better'n these folks deserve." He turned, like he meant to leave.

"I'll try to clear your name in this," Gabe said, his voice almost too weak to be heard. "I saw Cleve draw first, and so did everybody else. I'll tell Judge Green."

The gunman hesitated, looking to the south. "It don't make a hell of a lot of difference now," he replied. "Besides, it's warmer down where I'm headed. Best of luck to you, Sheriff Miller."

As Ramsey walked toward his horse, Peggy Sue raced down the steps to her father. More onlookers came, sensing that the danger had passed. Peggy Sue's sobbing drowned out the sound of Gabe's voice when he asked Martha to drive the wagon over. "I'm not real sure I can walk that far," he added in a whisper.

Just as Martha was hurrying off, Carl Jones trotted over to Gabe and crouched down beside him. "We can take my buggy over to Gatesville, Sheriff," he said. "It'll be a lot faster."

Gabe could barely manage a nod and a weak, "Thanks, Carl," as the saloonkeeper helped him to sit up. Blinking, trying to clear his head, Gabe was distracted by the sounds of a horse.

Buck Ramsey galloped his roan past the church, sitting ramrod straight in the saddle. Gabe watched him ride off with a mixture of feelings. In most respects, he was glad to see such a dangerous man leave this part of the country. Folks would sleep better now. Yet, Gabe also viewed the gunman's departure with a touch of sadness.

Ramsey's family rested below the ground here in Coryell County, and it was doubtful he would ever return to visit their graves. Gabe promised himself that he would try to find Anna Ramsey's bones out at the Wade ranch so she could be buried beside Johnny. It wasn't much more than a gesture, but he would do it if he could.

Clutching his aching ribs, he touched something in his inside coat pocket as Carl hurried off to get the buggy. The tintype of Anna Ramsey was there, and he knew Buck would have wanted it. But when he looked down the road the gunman had ridden, the road was empty. "Sorry I forgot about this," he muttered, as though he'd spoken to Ramsey just then.

His hand was trembling with pain and weakness when he took the likeness from his pocket. For a time he simply stared at it, marveling at Anna's unusual beauty. Cleve's lust for her had set off a chain of ugly events here in Eagle Springs a decade earlier . . . events that had remained a secret until now. Gabe knew folks would have plenty to talk about in the years ahead, recalling the Sunday before Christmas when the killer's identity was uncovered.

He turned his head when the sounds of Peggy Sue's crying invaded his thoughts. She too had been a victim. Motherless, and now fatherless. Her memories of her father tainted by his hideous crime and his violent end.

Harlan Huffman walked up, taking Gabe's attention from Peggy Sue. Harlan knelt down with concern in his eyes. "You gonna be all right, Gabriel?" he asked, glancing down at the blood seeping through Gabe's shirt.

"I reckon," he replied. "It hurts something awful, but I reckon I'll live."

"We wouldn't want to lose you," Harlan said, touching Gabe's shoulder. "When you're feelin' better, you'll have to tell us the whole story."

Gabe looked down at the tintype. "This was part of what I found. It was in Cleve's attic, at the bottom of an old trunk, along with a bunch of letters Buck had written home during the war. It proves the trunk belonged to Anna Ramsey. Cleve admitted that he killed Johnny and kidnapped Mrs. Ramsey. After she died he buried her out behind the house. He told me just before he tried to kill me."

"I swear, then it was Cleve who shot you," Harlan said softly, like he still couldn't quite believe it, glancing down at the likeness. Then he looked at Gabe. "There's some of us who owe you an apology for not believin' you in the first place."

Gabe closed his eyes when a renewed wave of pain washed through him. "Don't worry about it."

Carl drove up in the buggy and with the help of Reverend Sims and Harlan, assisted Gabe into the buggy beside Martha. He settled into the seat and closed his eyes. As the buggy lurched away from the church, he felt Martha's palm against his face and did his best to smile.

CHAPTER 24

Early spring flowers danced back and forth on soft currents of air as Gabe leaned on the handle of his shovel, looking down the hill from a shady spot below a gnarled oak. Among the dark bluebonnets and golden Indian paintbrushes, meadowlarks flitted about, searching for seeds and insects. He surveyed the scene from the rear of the Wade mansion, finding himself in a somber mood, remembering a cold winter day in December when things here finally fell into place. At the bottom of the shallow hole he'd found the remains of Anna Marie Ramsey. Keeping a promise he'd made only to himself, he would bury her beside her son at the Eagle Springs cemetery. Sweat plastered his shirt to his back as he rested, looking down the slope, listening to the chirps and calls of wild birds, the larks and scissortails, bluejays and mockingbirds, and the occasional lyrical call of a whitewing dove from a distant tree branch.

A sound made him turn. Peggy Sue came

out of the house with a glass of lemonade. She smiled at him, balancing the drink in her hand. "You look tired," she said, offering him the glass when she arrived.

"I found her," he said quietly, pointing down to the hole. "Right where I thought she'd be, beside this big oak tree."

The girl wouldn't look down at the bones, casting a glance to the horizon. "I'll never understand why Pa did it," she said in a faraway voice.

"We'll never know," Gabe replied thoughtfully. Trying to change the subject, he said, "I don't know when Martha and I will ever pay back the money we borrowed from the bank to buy the Cummings farm. Now I'm up to my neck in debt. All my spare time's taken up, fixing that old house so the rain won't come in."

"I'm glad to have y'all as neighbors," Peggy Sue said, smiling. "Martha and I can gossip all summer long."

He looked at her then, returning her smile. "Thanks for the lemonade. If I don't get back to digging, it'll be dark before I'm done." He drained the rest of his drink.

She took his empty glass. "I often wonder what happened to that gunfighter," she said. "Nobody's ever heard where he went."

Gabe never told anyone about the letter

from Ramsey, not even Martha. It had come late in February, from Piedras Negras, below the Mexican border. After he got it, Gabe sent the tintype of Anna in care of the postmaster down there, along with a note saying that Judge Green had dismissed any charges against Ramsey for the shooting of Cleveland Wade, calling it self-defense. "It's hard to say," Gabe told Peggy Sue, looking south. "Maybe he went down to Mexico. There was nothing to keep him here. With his family dead and a bad reputation, I reckon he'd move on to someplace where nobody ever heard of him. He could start over down there if he had a mind to."

Just then the back door slammed at the rear of the Wade mansion. Gabe looked over his shoulder. Martha stepped off the back porch, smiling at the two of them.

"If I was the jealous type, I'd be worried," she said, heading for the tree where Gabe stood. "A handsome man and a beautiful girl almost always spells trouble." She gave him a mocking frown. "But I know this man, and the way to his heart is through his stomach. Lunch is almost ready. The muffins will be done in a minute or two."

He watched her come closer, wearing the summer dress she'd made from the yellow cloth he gave her after Christmas. A pair of

264

yellow bows fluttered in the wind, tied to her braids. He couldn't help but smile when he saw her, thinking how pretty she looked right then.

She halted beside Peggy Sue and looked down into the hole Gabe was digging. "You found her, didn't you?" she asked, taking a half step back, looking away quickly. "Let's go inside, Peggy Sue," she added softly.

Both women walked toward the house. "I'll be along in a minute," he said, frowning at the fragments of a purple dress he'd uncovered a moment ago, then pieces of a human skeleton. He dreaded finishing the grisly task.

Shaking his head, he gazed at the horizon, remembering Harvey Barnes. It had only been a few weeks before the old man died that Gabe was recovered sufficiently from his wound to ride over to Harvey's. He related to him the details of Johnny's and Anna's deaths, as much as he knew from what Cleve admitted that fateful day. Harvey's sunken face bore a look of contentment after he heard the story. Although he could barely manage to speak, he told Gabe how glad he was that the mystery had been solved.

Gabe recalled Cleve Wade's funeral, and the odd feeling he had afterward when Cleve was buried near Johnny Ramsey that justice finally had been served, after all. Buck Ramsey's brand of justice. Now there was only this one bit of unfinished business — to bury Anna beside her son — before Gabe could put the entire affair to rest. But he knew the memory of it would never go away completely in the hearts and minds of the people here.

For many Christmases to come, folks would remember the bloody killing in front of the church. On the surface, Eagle Springs appeared to be a quiet, peaceful place to the occasional travelers passing through. Only those who lived nearby knew about the town's darker side, its brief period of violence.

"Lunch is ready!" Martha called from the kitchen window, ending Gabe's wandering thoughts. He tossed the shovel aside and headed for the house.

Alone at the cemetery, he stared down at the simple headstone for a time, lost in memories. It didn't matter that he'd paid for the marker himself over at Gatesville when he learned that the county wouldn't bear the expense. The small stone read: *Anna Marie Ramsey*. He hadn't known the date of her birth, or the exact date of her death.

Standing with his hat in his hands, Gabe looked toward the ridge above Eagle Springs, remembering the day Buck Ramsey rode into town. That wintry December day had been the beginning of a time that would end with the most notorious day in the town's history. Gabe had been visited by newspaper reporters from almost every city within a hundred miles, asking him to recount the grim tale again and again. In particular, he was asked to relate every detail of the deadly duel between the notorious Buck Ramsey and Cleveland Wade.

It was from a newspaperman from Fort Worth that Gabe learned about Cleve's questionable past. Cleve had once been a gambler, frequenting the saloons of Hell's Half Acre in the heart of Fort Worth before the war, widely known for his inclination to cheat at cards when playing poker among the young cowboys headed up the cattle trails. So the story went, Cleve was suspected of robbing and killing a wealthy San Antonio cattleman one night, although the case against him could never be proven. He left town right after that with his infant daughter, born to a Hell's Half Acre prostitute who died giving birth to the child. (Gabe convinced the reporter to omit any mention of the prostitute from the story to save Peggy Sue further embarrassment.)

Gabe took one final look at Anna's grave, then donned his hat for the ride back home. It made no sense to dwell on what had happened. He had a future to think about, one that looked brighter now. Word had come to the gin that cotton buyers from England were in Galveston, offering good prices for bales ready to be shipped to Europe immediately. Last year's cotton was selling briskly to foreign markets, ending the terrible grip of Reconstruction on most farmers across the South. With the payment for last year's crop, Gabe and Martha could pay almost half the mortgage on the Cummings farm. Another good year or two, and they would own the land free and clear.

There was more good news — last week she had told him that the doctor over at Gatesville had confirmed that she was with child, and Gabe had never seen his wife any happier. Without admitting to it publicly, he shared her joy over the coming birth.

With gentle pressure from Gabe's heels, the colt struck a trot toward the top of the ridge above town. Spring grasses sprouted from the soil everywhere he looked. The hills and valleys had turned green almost overnight, blanketed with lush growth after the soil absorbed moisture from melted winter snows.

At the crest of the ridge, Gabe halted the chestnut to gaze across the valley where Justin Creek wound its way to the Leon. He smiled unconsciously when he saw the town below. He knew he could expect to hold the sheriff's job here as long as he wanted, after his role in solving the town's long-standing mystery. The idea struck his fancy. He was suited for the job.

He kicked the colt to a short lope and started down the hill, eager to see Martha at suppertime. There was spring plowing to be done when he got home. The time had finally come to stop digging graves and to begin planting seeds around Coryell County. Though he held down a part-time sheriff's job, Gabe Miller was, at heart, still a farmer.

We hope you have enjoyed this Large Print book. Other Thorndike Press or Chivers Press Large Print books are available at your library or directly from the publishers. For more information about current and upcoming titles, please call or write, without obligation, to:

Thorndike Press
P.O. Box 159
Thorndike, Maine 04986
USA
Tel. (800) 223-6121
(207) 948-2962
(in Maine and Canada, call collect)

OR

Chivers Press Limited
Windsor Bridge Road
Bath BA2 3AX
England
Tel. (0225) 335336

All our Large Print titles are designed for easy reading, and all our books are made to last.